Paul and Virginia

Paul and Virginia

BERNARDIN DE SAINT PIERRE

Translated by Helen Maria Williams

WILDSIDE PRESS
Doylestown, Pennsylvania

1851

Prepared from an edition published by
Appleton and Company of New York.

Paul and Virginia
A publication of
WILDSIDE PRESS
P.O. Box 301
Holicong, PA 18928-0301

www.wildsidepress.com

Preface

The following translation of "Paul and Virginia,"
was written at Paris, amidst the horrors of Robe-
spierre's tyranny. During that gloomy epocha it was
difficult to find occupations which might cheat the
days of calamity of their weary length. Society had
vanished; and amidst the minute vexations of Jacobini-
cal despotism, which, while it murdered in *mass*, persecuted in detail, the resources of writing, and even
reading, were encompassed with danger. The researches
of domiciliary visits had already compelled me to
commit to the flames a manuscript volume, where I
had traced the political scenes of which I had been a
witness, with the coloring of their first impressions on
my mind, with those fresh tints that fade from recollection; and since my pen, accustomed to follow the
impulse of my feelings, could only have drawn, at that
fatal period, those images of desolation and despair
which haunted my imagination, and dwelt upon my
heart, writing was forbidden employment. Even reading had its perils; for books had sometimes aristocrati-
cal insignia, and sometimes counter revolutionary al-
lusions; and when the administrators of police hap-

pened to think the writer a conspirator, they punished the reader as his accomplice.

In this situation I gave myself the task of employing a few hours every day in translating the charming little novel of Bernardin St. Pierre, entitled "Paul and Virginia;" and I found the most soothing relief in wandering from my own gloomy reflections to those enchanting scenes of the Mauritius, which he has so admirably described. I also composed a few Sonnets adapted to the peculiar productions of that part of the globe, which are interspersed in the work. Some, indeed, are lost, as well as a part of the translation, which I have since supplied, having been sent to the Municipality of Paris, in order to be examined as English papers; where they still remain, mingled with revolutionary placards, motions, and harangues; and are not likely to be restored to my possession.

With respect to the translation, I can only hope to deserve the humble merit of not having deformed the beauty of the original. I have, indeed, taken one liberty with my author, which it is fit I should acknowledge, that of omitting several pages of general observations, which, however excellent in themselves, would be passed over with impatience by the English reader, when they interrupt the pathetic narrative. In this respect, the two nations seem to change characters; and while the serious and reflecting Englishman requires, in novel writing, as well as on the theater, a rapid succession of incidents, much bustle and stage effect, without suffering the author to appear himself, and stop the progress of the story; the gay and restless Frenchman listens attentively to long philosophical reflections, while the catastrophe of the drama hangs in suspense.

My last poetical productions (the Sonnets which are interspersed in this work) may perhaps be found even more imperfect than my earlier compositions; since, after a long exile from England, I can scarcely flatter myself that my ear is become more attuned to the harmony of a language, with the sounds of which it is seldom gladdened; or that my poetical taste is improved by living in a country where arts have given place to arms. But the public will, perhaps, receive with indulgence a work written under such peculiar circumstances; not composed in the calm of literary leisure, or in pursuit of literary fame, but amidst the turbulence of the most cruel sensations, and in order to escape awhile from overwhelming misery.

HELEN MARIA WILLIAMS

Paul and Virginia

O n the eastern coast of the mountain which rises above Port Louis in the Mauritius, upon a piece of land bearing the marks of former cultivation, are seen the ruins of two small cottages. Those ruins are situated near the center of a valley, formed by immense rocks, and which opens only towards the north. On the left rises the mountain, called the Height of Discovery, from whence the eye marks the distant sail when it first touches the verge of the horizon, and whence the signal is given when a vessel approaches the island. At the foot of this mountain stands the town of Port Louis. On the right is formed the road, which stretches from Port Louis to the Shaddock Grove, where the church, bearing that name, lifts its head, surrounded by its avenues of bamboo, in the midst of a spacious plain; and the prospect terminates in a forest extending to the furthest bounds of the island. The front view presents the bay, denominated the Bay of the Tomb: a little on the right is seen the Cape of Misfortune; and beyond rolls the expanded ocean, on the surface of which appear a few uninhabited islands, and, among others, the Point of Endeavor, which resembles a bastion built upon the flood.

At the entrance of the valley which presents those various objects, the echoes of the mountain incessantly repeat the hollow murmurs of the winds that shake the neighboring forests, and the tumultuous dashing of the waves which break at a distance upon the cliffs. But near the ruined cottages all is calm and still, and the only objects which there meet the eye are rude steep rocks, that rise like a surrounding rampart. Large clumps of trees grow at their base, on their rifted sides, and even on their majestic tops, where the clouds seem to repose. The showers, which their bold points attract, often paint the vivid colors of the rainbow on their green and brown declivities, and swell the sources of the little river which flows at their feet, called the river of Fan-Palms.

Within this enclosure reigns the most profound silence. The waters, the air, all the elements are at peace. Scarcely does the echo repeat the whispers of the palm trees spreading their broad leaves, the long points of which are gently balanced by the winds. A soft light illuminates the bottom of this deep valley, on which the sun only shines at noon. But even at break of day the rays of light are thrown on the surrounding rocks; and the sharp peaks, rising above the shadows of the mountain, appear like tints of gold and purple gleaming upon the azure sky.

To this scene I loved to resort, where I might enjoy at once the richness of the extensive landscape, and the charm of uninterrupted solitude. One day, when I was seated at the foot of the cottages, and contemplating their ruins, a man, advanced in years, passed near the spot. He was dressed in the ancient garb of the island, his feet were bare, and he leaned upon a staff of ebony: his hair was white, and the expression of his countenance was dignified and interesting. I bowed to him with respect; he returned the salutation: and, after looking at me with some earnestness, came and placed himself upon the hillock where I was seated. Encouraged by this mark of confidence, I thus addressed him: —

"Father, can you tell me to whom those cottages once belonged?" "My son," replied the old man, "those heaps of rubbish, and that unfilled land, were, twenty years ago, the property of two families, who then found happiness in this solitude. Their history is affecting; but what European, pursuing his way to the Indies, will pause one moment to interest himself in the fate of a few obscure individuals? What European can picture happiness to his imagination amidst poverty and neglect? The curiosity of mankind is only attracted by the history of the great; and yet from that knowledge little use can be derived." "Father," I rejoined, "from your manners and your observations, I perceive that you have acquired much experience of human life. If you have leisure, relate to me, I beseech you, the history of the ancient inhabitants of this desert; and be assured, that even the men who are most perverted by the prejudices of the world, find a soothing pleasure in contemplating that happiness which belongs to simplicity and virtue." The old man, after a short silence, during which he leaned his face upon his hands, as if he were trying to recall the images of the past, thus began his narration: —

"Monsieur de la Tour, a young man who was a native of Normandy, after having in vain solicited a commission in the French Army, or some support from his own family, at length determined to seek his fortune in this island, where he arrived in 1726. He brought hither a young woman whom he loved tenderly, and by whom he was no less tenderly beloved. She belonged to a rich and ancient family of the same province; but

he had married her without fortune, and in opposition
to the will of her relations, who refused their consent,
because he was found guilty of being descended from
parents who had no claims to nobility. Monsieur de
la Tour, leaving his wife at Port Louis, embarked for
Madagascar, in order to purchase a few slaves to assist
him in forming a plantation in this island. He landed
at that unhealthy season which commences about the
middle of October: and soon after his arrival died of
the pestilential fever, which prevails in that country six
months of the year, and which will forever baffle the
attempts of the European nations to form establishments on that fatal soil. His effects were seized
upon by the rapacity of strangers; and his wife, who
was pregnant, found herself a widow in a country
where she had neither credit nor recommendation, and
no earthly possession, or rather support, save one
Negro woman. Too delicate to solicit protection or
relief from any other man after the death of him whom
alone she loved, misfortune armed her with courage,
and she resolved to cultivate with her slave a little spot
of ground, and procure for herself the means of sub-
sistence. In an island almost a desert, and where the
ground was left to the choice of the settler, she avoided
those spots which were most fertile and most favorable
to commerce; and seeking some nook of the mountain,
some secret asylum, where she might live solitary and
unknown, she bent her way from the town towards
those rocks, where she wished to shelter herself as in a
nest. All suffering creatures, from a sort of common
instinct, fly for refuge amidst their pains to haunts the
most wild and desolate; as if rocks could form a rampart against misfortune; as if the calm of nature could
hush the tumults of the soul. That Providence, which
lends its support when we ask but the supply of our
necessary wants, had a blessing in reserve for Madame

de la Tour, which neither riches nor greatness can purchase; this blessing was a friend.

"The spot to which Madame de la Tour fled had already been inhabited a year by a young woman of a lively, good natured, and affectionate disposition. Margaret (for that was her name) was born in Brittany, of a family of peasants, by whom she was cherished and beloved, and with whom she might have passed life in simple rustic happiness, if, misled by the weakness of a tender heart, she had not listened to the passion of a gentleman in the neighborhood, who promised her marriage. He soon abandoned her, and adding inhumanity to seduction, refused to ensure a provision for the child of which she was pregnant. Margaret then determined to leave forever her native village, and go, where her fault might be concealed, to some colony distant from that country where she had lost the only portion of a poor peasant girl — her reputation. With some borrowed money she purchased an old Negro slave, with whom she cultivated a little spot of this canton. Here Madame de la Tour, followed by her Negro woman, found Margaret suckling her child. Soothed by the sight of a person in a situation somewhat similar to her own, Madame de la Tour related, in a few words, her past condition and her present wants. Margaret was deeply affected by the recital; and, more anxious to excite confidence than esteem, she confessed, without disguise, the errors of which she had been guilty. 'As for me,' said she, 'I deserve my fate: but you, madam — you! at once virtuous and unhappy —' And, sobbing, she offered Madame de la Tour both her hut and her friendship. That lady, affected by this tender reception, pressed her in her arms, and exclaimed, 'Ah, surely Heaven will put an end to my misfortunes, since it inspires you, to whom I am a stranger, with more goodness towards me than I have ever experienced from my own relations!'

"I knew Margaret; and, although my habitation is a league and a half from hence, in the woods behind that sloping mountain, I considered myself as her neighbor. In the cities of Europe a street, sometimes even a less distance, separates families whom nature had united; but in new colonies we consider those persons as neighbors from whom we are divided only by woods and mountains; and above all, at that period when this island had little intercourse with the Indies, neighborhood alone gave a claim to friendship, and hospitality toward strangers seemed less a duty than a pleasure. No sooner was I informed that Margaret had found a companion, than I hastened thither, in hope of being useful to my neighbor and her guest.

"Madame de la Tour possessed all those melancholy graces which give beauty additional power, by blending sympathy with admiration. Her figure was interesting, and her countenance expressed at once dignity and dejection. She appeared to be in the last stage of her pregnancy. I told them that, for the future interests of their children, and to prevent the intrusion of any other settler, it was necessary they should divide between them the property of this wild sequestered valley, which is nearly twenty acres in extent. They confided that task to me, and I marked out two equal portions of land. One includes the higher part of this enclosure, from, the peak of that rock buried in clouds, whence springs the rapid river of Fan-Palms, to that wide cleft which you see on the summit of the mountain, and which is called the Cannon's Mouth, from the resemblance in its form. It is difficult to find a path along this wild portion of enclosure, the soil of which is encumbered with fragments of rock, or worn into channels formed by torrents; yet it produces noble trees, and innumerable fountains and rivulets. The other portion of land is comprised in the plain extending along the banks of the river of Fan-Palms, to the opening where we are now seated, from whence the river takes its course between those two hills, until it falls into the sea. You may still trace the vestiges of some meadow-land; and this part of the common is less rugged, but not more valuable than the other; since in the rainy season it becomes marshy, and in dry weather is so hard and unbending, that it will yield only to the stroke of the hatchet. When I had thus divided the property, I persuaded my neighbors to draw lots for their separate possessions. The higher portion of land became the property of Madame de la Tour; the lower, of Margaret; and each seemed satisfied with her respective share. They entreated me to place their habitations together, that they might at all times enjoy the soothing intercourse of friendship, and the consolation of mutual kind offices. Margaret's cottage was situated near the center of the valley, and just on the boundary of her own plantation. Close to that spot I built another cottage for the dwelling of Madame de la Tour: and thus the two friends, while they possessed all the advantages of neighborhood, lived on their own property. I myself cut palisades from the mountain, and brought leaves of Fan-Palms from the seashore, in order to construct those two cottages, of which you can now discern neither the entrance nor the roof. Yet, alas! there still remain but too many traces for my remembrance! Time, which so rapidly destroys the proud monuments of empires, seems in this desert to spare those of friendship, as if to perpetuate my regrets to the last hour of my existence.

"Scarcely was her cottage finished, when Madame de la Tour was delivered of a girl. I had been the godfather of Margaret's child, who was christened by the name of Paul. Madame de la Tour desired me to perform the same office for her child also, together with her friend, who gave her the name of Virginia. 'She will be virtuous,' cried Margaret, 'and she will be happy. I have only known misfortune by wandering from virtue.'

"At the time Madame de la Tour recovered, those two little territories had already begun to yield some produce, perhaps in a small degree owing to the care which I occasionally bestowed on their improvement, but far more to the indefatigable labors of the two slaves. Margaret's slave, who was called Domingo, was still healthy and robust, although advanced in years: he possessed some knowledge, and a good natural understanding. He cultivated indiscriminately, on both settlements, such spots of ground as were most fertile, and sowed whatever grain he thought most congenial to each particular soil. Where the ground was poor, he strewed maize; where it was most fruitful, he planted wheat; and rice in such spots as were marshy. He threw the seeds of gourds and cucumbers at the foot of the rocks, which they loved to climb, and decorate with their luxuriant foliage. In dry spots he cultivated the sweet potato; the cotton tree flourished upon the heights, and the sugar-cane grew in the clayey soil. He reared some plants of coffee on the hills, where the grain, although small, is excellent. The plantain trees, which spread their grateful shade on the banks of the river, and encircled the cottage, yielded fruit throughout the year. And, lastly, Domingo cultivated a few plants of tobacco, to charm away his own cares. Sometimes he was employed in cutting wood for firing from the mountain, sometimes in hewing pieces of rock within the enclosure, in order to level the paths. He was much attached to Margaret, and not less to Madame de la Tour, whose woman-woman, Mary, he had married at the time of Virginia's birth; and he was passionately fond of his wife. Mary was born at Madagascar, from whence she had brought a few arts of industry. She could weave baskets, and a sort of stuff, with long grass that grows in the woods. She was active, cleanly, and, above all, faithful. It was her care to prepare their meals, to rear the poultry, and go sometimes to Port Louis, and sell the superfluities of these little plantations, which were not very considerable. If you add to the personages I have already mentioned two goats, who were brought up with the children, and a great dog, who kept watch at night, you will have a complete idea of the household, as well as of the revenue of those two farms.

"Madame de la Tour and her friend were employed from the morning till the evening in spinning cotton for the use of their families. Destitute of all those things which their own industry could not supply, they walked about their habitations with their feet bare, and shoes were a convenience reserved for Sunday, when, at an early hour, they attended mass at the church of the Shaddock Grove, which you see yonder. That church is far more distant than Port Louis; yet they seldom visited the town, lest they should be treated with contempt, because they were dressed in the coarse blue linen of Bengal, which is usually worn by slaves. But is there in that external deference which fortune commands a compensation for domestic happiness? If they had something to suffer from the world, this served but to endear their humble home. No sooner did Mary and Domingo perceive them from this elevated spot, on the road of the Shaddock Grove, than they flew to the foot of the mountain, in order to help them to ascend. They discerned in the looks of their domestics that joy which their return inspired. They found in their retreat neatness, independence, all those blessings which are the recompense of toil, and received those services which have their source in affection. — United by the tie of similar wants, and the sympathy of similar misfortunes, they gave each other the tender names of companion, friend, sister. — They had but one will, one interest, one table. All their possessions were in common. And if sometimes a passion more ardent than friendship awakened in their hearts the pang of unavailing anguish, a pure religion, united with chaste manners, drew their affections towards another life; as the trembling flame rises towards heaven, when it no longer finds any aliment on earth.

"Madame de la Tour sometimes, leaving the household cares to Margaret, wandered out alone; and, amidst the sublime scenery, indulged that luxury of pensive sadness, which is so soothing to the mind after the first emotions of turbulent sorrow have subsided. Sometimes she poured forth the effusions of melancholy in the language of verse; and, although her compositions have little poetical merit, they appear to me to bear the marks of genuine sensibility. Many of her poems are lost; but some still remain in my possession, and a few still hang on my memory. I will repeat to you a sonnet addressed to Love.

SONNET
TO LOVE

Ah, Love! ere yet I knew thy fatal power,
Bright glow'd the color of my youthful days,
As, on the sultry zone, the torrid rays,
That paint the broad-leaved plantain's glossy bower;
Calm was my bosom as this silent hour,

When o'er the deep, scarce heard, the zephyr strays,
'Midst the cool tam'rinds indolently plays,
Nor from the orange shakes its od'rous flower:
But, ah! since Love has all my heart possess'd,
That desolated heart what sorrows tear!
Disturb'd and wild as ocean's troubled breast,
When the hoarse tempest of the night is there
Yet my complaining spirit asks no rest;
This bleeding bosom cherishes despair.

"The tender and sacred duties which nature imposed, became a source of additional happiness to those affectionate mothers, whose mutual friendship acquired new strength at the sight of their children, alike the offspring of unhappy love. They delighted to place their infants together in the same bath, to nurse them in the same cradle, and sometimes changed the maternal bosom at which they received nourishment, as if to blend with the ties of friendship that instinctive affection which this act produces.

'My friend,' cried Madame de la Tour, 'we shall each of us have two children, and each of our children will have two mothers.' As two buds which remain on two trees of the same kind, after the tempest has broken all their branches, produce more delicious fruit, if each, separated from the maternal stem, be grafted on the neighboring tree; so those two children, deprived of all other support, imbibed sentiments more tender than those of son and daughter, brother and sister, when exchanged at the breast of those who had given them birth. While they were yet in their cradle, their mothers talked of their marriage; and this prospect of conjugal felicity, with which they soothed their own cares, often called forth the tears of bitter regret. The misfortunes of one mother had arisen from having neglected marriage, those of the other from having submitted to its

laws: one had been made unhappy by attempting to
raise herself above her humble condition of life, the
other by descending from her rank. But they found
consolation in reflecting that their more fortunate
children, far from the cruel prejudices of Europe, those
prejudices which poison the most precious sources of
our happiness, would enjoy at once the pleasures of
love and the blessings of equality.

"Nothing could exceed that attachment which those
infants already displayed for each other. If Paul com-
plained, his mother pointed to Virginia; and at that
sight he smiled, and was appeased. If any accident
befell Virginia, the cries of Paul gave notice of the
disaster; and then Virginia would suppress her com-
plaints when she found that Paul was unhappy. When
I came hither, I usually found them quite naked, which
is the custom of this country, tottering in their walk,
and holding each other by the hands and under the
arms, as we represent the constellation of the Twins.
At night these infants often refused to be separated,
and were found lying in the same cradle, their cheeks,
their bosoms pressed close together, their hands
thrown round each other's neck, and sleeping, locked
in one another's arms.

"When they began to speak, the first names they
learnt to give each other were those of brother and
sister, and childhood knows no softer appellation.
Their education served to augment their early friendship, by directing it to the supply of their reciprocal
wants. In a short time, all that regarded the household
economy, the care of preparing the rural repasts, became the task of Virginia, whose labors were always
crowned with the praises and kisses of her brother. As
for Paul, always in motion, he dug the garden with
Domingo, or followed him with a little hatchet into
the woods, where, if in his rambles he espied a beautiful

flower, fine fruit, or a nest of birds, even at the top of a tree, he climbed up, and brought it home to his sister.

"When you met with one of these children, you might be sure the other was not distant. One day, coming down that mountain, I saw Virginia at the end of the garden, running toward the house, with her petticoat thrown over her head, in order to screen herself from a shower of rain. At a distance, I thought she was alone; but as I hastened towards her, in order to help her on, I perceived that she held Paul by the arm, who was almost entirely enveloped in the same cavity, and both were laughing heartily at being sheltered together under an umbrella of their own invention. Those two charming faces, placed within the petticoat, swelled by the wind, recalled to my mind the children of Leda, enclosed within the same shell.

"Their sole study was how to please and assist each other; for of all other things they were ignorant, and knew neither how to read nor write. They were never disturbed by researches into past times, nor did their curiosity extend beyond the bounds of that mountain. They believed the world ended at the shores of their own island, and all their ideas and affections were confined within its limits. Their mutual tenderness, and that of their mothers, employed all the activity of their souls. Their tears had never been called forth by long application to useless sciences. Their minds had never been wearied by lessons of morality, superfluous to bosoms unconscious of ill. They had never been taught that they must not steal, because everything with them was in common; or be intemperate, because their simple food was left to their own discretion; or false, because they had no truth to conceal. Their young imaginations had never been terrified by the idea that God has punishments in store for ungrateful children, since with them filial affection arose naturally from maternal fondness. All they had been taught of religion was to love it; and if they did not offer up long prayers in the church, wherever they were, in the house, in the fields, in the woods, they raised towards heaven their innocent hands, and their hearts purified by virtuous affections.

"Thus passed their early childhood, like a beautiful dawn, the prelude of a bright day. Already they partook with their mothers the cares of the household. As soon as the cry of the wakeful cock announced the first beam of the morning, Virginia arose, and hastened to draw water from a neighboring spring; then returning to the house, she prepared the breakfast. When the rising sun lighted up the points of those rocks which overhang this enclosure, Margaret and her child went to the dwelling of Madame de la Tour, and they offered up together their morning prayer. This sacrifice of thanksgiving always preceded their first repast, which they often partook before the door of the cottage, seated upon the grass, under a canopy of plantain; and while the branches of that delightful tree afforded a grateful shade, its solid fruit furnished food ready prepared by nature; and its long glossy leaves, spread upon the table, supplied the want of linen.

"Plentiful and wholesome nourishment gave early growth and vigor to the persons of those children, and their countenances expressed the purity and peace of their souls. At twelve years of age the figure of Virginia was in some degree formed: a profusion of light hair shaded her face, to which her blue eyes and coral lips gave the most charming brilliancy. Her eyes sparkled with vivacity when she spoke; but when she was silent, her look had a cast upwards, which gave it an expression of extreme sensibility, or rather of tender melancholy. Already the figure of Paul displayed the graces of manly beauty. He was taller than Virginia; his skin was of a darker tint; his nose more aquiline; and his black eyes would have been too piercing, if the long eyelashes, by which were shaded, had not given them a look of softness. He was constantly in motion, except when his sister appeared; and then, placed at her side, he became quiet. Their meals often passed in silence, and, from the grace of their attitudes, the beautiful proportions of their figures, and their naked feet, you might have fancied you beheld an antique group of white marble, representing some of the children of Niobe; if those eyes which sought to meet those smiles which were answered by smiles of the most tender softness, had not rather given you the idea of those happy celestial spirits, whose nature is love, and who are not obliged to have recourse to words for the expression of that intuitive sentiment. In the meantime, Madame de la Tour, perceiving every day some unfolding grace, some new beauty, in her daughter, felt her maternal anxiety increase with her tenderness. She often said to me, 'If I should die, what will become of Virginia without fortune?'

"Madame de la Tour had an aunt in France, who was a woman of quality, rich, old and a great bigot. She had behaved towards her niece with so much cruelty upon her marriage that Madame de la Tour had determined that no distress or misfortune should ever compel her to have recourse to her hard-hearted relation. But when she became a mother, the pride of resentment was stilled in the stronger feelings of maternal tenderness. She wrote to her aunt, informing her of the sudden death of her husband, the birth of her daughter, and the difficulties in which she was involved at a distance from her own country, without support, and burdened with a child. She received no answer; but, notwithstanding that high spirit which was natural to her character, she no longer feared exposing herself to mortification and reproach; and, although she knew her relation would never pardon her for having married a man of merit, but not of noble birth, she continued to write to her by every opportunity, in the hope of awakening her compassion for Virginia. Many years, however, passed, during which she received not the smallest testimony of her remembrance.

"At length, in 1738, three years after the arrival of Monsieur de la Bourdonnais in this island, Madame de la Tour was informed that the governor had a letter to give her from her aunt. She flew to Port Louis, careless on this occasion of appearing in her homely garment. Maternal hope and joy subdued all those little considerations, which are lost when the mind is absorbed by any powerful sentiment. Monsieur de la Bourdonnais delivered to her a letter from her aunt, who informed her, that she deserved her fate for having married an adventurer and a libertine; that misplaced passions brought along with them their own punishment, and that the sudden death of her husband must be considered as a visitation from heaven; that she had done well in going to a distant island, rather than dishonor her family by remaining in France: and that, after all, in the colony where she had taken refuge, every person grew rich except the idle. Having thus lavished sufficient censure upon the conduct of her niece, she finished by a eulogium on herself. To avoid, she said, the almost inevitable evils of marriage, she had determined to remain in a single state. In truth, being of a very ambitious temper, she had resolved only to unite, herself to a man of high rank; and although she; was very rich, her fortune was not found a sufficient bribe, even at court, to counterbalance the malignant dispositions of her mind, and the disagreeable qualities of her person.

"She added, in a postscript, that, after mature deliberation, she had strongly recommended her niece to Monsieur de la Bourdonnais. This she had indeed done, but in a manner of late too common, and which renders a patron perhaps even more formidable than a declared enemy: for, in order to justify herself, she had cruelly slandered her niece, while she affected to pity her misfortunes.

"Madame de la Tour, whom no unprejudiced person could have seen without feeling sympathy and respect, was received with the utmost coolness by Monsieur de la Bourdonnais; and when she painted to him her own situation, and that of her child, he replied, 'We will see what can be done — there are so many to relieve — why did you affront so respectable a relation? — You have been much to blame.'

"Madame de la Tour returned to her cottage, her bosom throbbing with all the bitterness of disappointment. When she arrived, she threw herself on a chair, and then flinging her aunt's letter on the table, exclaimed to her friend, 'This is the recompense of eleven years of patient expectation!' As Madame de la Tour was the only person in the little circle who could read, she again took up the letter, which she read aloud. Scarcely had she finished, when Margaret exclaimed, 'What have we to do with your relations? Has God then forsaken us? He only is our father! Have we not hitherto been happy? Why then this regret? You have no courage.' Seeing Madame de la Tour in tears, she threw herself upon her neck, and pressing her in her arms, 'My dear friend!' cried she, 'my dear friend!' But her emotion choked her utterance.

"At this sight Virginia burst into tears, and pressed her mother's hand and Margaret's alternately to her lips and to her heart: while Paul, with his eyes inflamed with anger, cried, clasped his hands together, and stamped with his feet, not knowing whom to blame for this scene of misery. The noise soon led Domingo and Mary to the spot, and the little habitation resounded with the cries of distress. Ah, Madame! — My good mistress! — My dear mother! — Do not weep!'

"Those tender proofs of affection at length dispelled Madame de la Tour's sorrow. She took Paul and Virginia in her arms, and, embracing them, cried, 'You are the cause of my affliction, and yet my only source of delight! Yes, my dear children, misfortune has reached me from a distance, but surely I am surrounded by happiness.' Paul and Virginia did not understand this reflection; but, when they saw that she was calm, they smiled, and continued to caress her. Thus tranquility was restored, and what had passed proved but a transient storm, which serves to give fresh verdure to a beautiful spring.

"Although Madame de la Tour appeared calm in the presence of her family, she sometimes communicated to me the feelings that preyed upon her mind, and soon after this period gave me the following sonnet: —

SONNET
TO DISAPPOINTMENT

Pale Disappointment! at thy freezing name
Chill fears in every shivering vein I prove;
My sinking pulse almost forgets to move,
And life almost forsakes my languid frame:
Yet thee, relentless nymph! no more I blame:
Why do my thoughts 'midst vain illusions rove?
Why gild the charms of friendship and of love

With the warm glow of fancy's purple flame?
When ruffling winds have some bright fane o'er-
     thrown,
Which shone on painted clouds, or seem'd to shine,
Shall the fond gazer dream for him alone
Those clouds were stable, and at fate repine?
I feel alas! the fault is all my own,
And, ah! the cruel punishment is mine!

"The amiable disposition of those children unfolded itself daily. On a Sunday, their mothers having gone at break of day to mass, at the church of the Shaddock Grove, the children perceived a Negro woman beneath the plantains which shaded their habitation. She appeared almost wasted to a skeleton, and had no other garment than a shred of coarse cloth thrown across her loins. She flung herself at Virginia's feet, who was preparing the family breakfast, and cried, 'My good young lady, have pity on a poor slave. For a whole month I have wandered amongst these mountains, half dead with hunger, and often pursued by the hunters and their dogs. I fled from my master, a rich planter of the Black River, who has used me as you see;' and she showed her body marked by deep scars from the lashes she had received. She added, 'I was going to drown myself; but hearing you lived here, I said to myself, since there are still some good white people in this country, I need not die yet.'

"Virginia answered with emotion, 'Take courage, Unfortunate creature! here is food,' and she gave her the breakfast she had prepared, which the poor slave in a few minutes devoured. When her hunger was appeased, Virginia said to her, 'Unhappy woman! will you let me go and ask forgiveness for you of your master? Surely the sight of you will touch him with pity. — Will you show me the way?' — 'Angel of heaven!' answered the poor Negro woman, 'I will follow you where you please.' Virginia called her brother, and begged him to accompany her. The slave led the way, by winding and difficult paths, through the woods, over mountains which they climbed with difficulty, and across rivers, through which they were obliged to wade. At length they reached the foot of a precipice upon the borders of the Black River. There they perceived a well-built house, surrounded by extensive plantations, and a great number of slaves employed at their various labors. Their master was walking amongst them with a pipe in his mouth, and a switch in his hand. He was a tall thin figure, of a brown complexion; his eyes were sunk in his head, and his dark eyebrows were joined together. Virginia, holding Paul by the hand, drew near, and with much emotion begged him, for the love of God, to pardon his poor slave, who stood trembling a few paces behind. The man at first paid little attention to the children, who, he saw, were meanly dressed. But when he observed the elegance of Virginia's form, and the profusion of her beautiful light tresses, which had escaped from beneath her blue cap; when he heard the soft tone of her voice, which trembled, as well as her own frame, while she implored his compassion; he took the pipe from his mouth, and lifting up his stick, swore, with a terrible oath, that he pardoned his slave, not for the love of Heaven, but of her who asked his forgiveness. Virginia made a sign to the slave to approach her master, and instantly sprung away, followed by Paul.

"They climbed up the precipice they had descended; and, having gained the summit, seated themselves at the foot of a tree, overcome with fatigue, hunger, and thirst. They had left their cottage fasting, and had walked five leagues since break of day. Paul said to Virginia, 'My dear sister, it is past noon, and I am sure you are thirsty and hungry; we shall find no dinner here; let us go down the mountain again, and ask the master of the poor slave for some food.' — 'Oh no,' answered Virginia; 'he frightens me too much. Remember what mamma sometimes says, the bread of the wicked is like stones in the mouth.' — 'What shall we do then?' said Paul: 'these trees produce no fruit; and I shall not be able to find even a tamarind or a lemon to refresh you.' Scarcely had he pronounced these words, when they heard the dashing of waters which fell from a neighboring rock. They ran thither, and having quenched their thirst at this crystal spring, they gathered a few cresses which grew on the border of the stream. While they were wandering in the woods in search of more solid nourishment, Virginia spied a young palm tree. The kind of cabbage which is found at the top of this tree, enfolded within its leaves, forms an excellent sustenance; but, although the stalk of the tree was not thicker than a man's leg, it was above sixty feet in height. The wood of this tree is composed of fine filaments; but the bark is so hard that it turns the edge of the hatchet, and Paul was not even furnished with a knife. At length he thought of setting fire to the palm tree, but a new difficulty occurred, he had no steel with which to strike fire; and, although the whole island is covered with rocks, I do not believe it is possible to find a flint. Necessity, however, is fertile in expedients, and the most useful inventions have arisen from men placed in the most destitute situations. Paul determined to kindle a fire in the manner of the Negroes. With the sharp end of a stone he made a small hole in the branch of a tree that was quite dry, which he held between his feet; he then sharpened another dry branch of a different sort of wood, and afterwards placing the piece of pointed wood in the small hole of the branch which he held with his feet, and turning it

rapidly between his hands, in a few minutes smoke and
sparks of fire issued from the points of contact. Paul
then heaped together dried grass and branches, and set
fire to the palm tree, which soon fell to the ground.
The fire was useful to him in stripping off the long,
thick and pointed leaves, within which the cabbage was
enclosed.

"Paul and Virginia ate part of the cabbage raw, and
part dressed upon the ashes, which they found equally
palatable. They made this frugal repast with delight,
from the remembrance of the benevolent action they
had performed in the morning: yet their joy was em-
bittered by the thoughts of that uneasiness which their
long absence would give their mothers. Virginia often
recurred to this subject: but Paul, who felt his strength
renewed by their meal, assured her that it would not
be long before they reached home.

"After dinner they recollected that they had no
guide, and that they were ignorant of the way. Paul,
whose spirit was not subdued by difficulties, said to
Virginia, 'The sun shines full upon our huts at noon:
we must pass as we did this morning, over that mountain with its three points, which you see yonder. Come,
let us go.' This mountain is called the Three Peaks. Paul
and Virginia descended the precipice of the Black
River, on the northern side; and arrived, after an hour's
walk, on the banks of a large stream.

"Great part of this island is so little known, even
now, that many of its rivers and mountains have not
yet received a name. The river, on the banks of which
our travelers stood, rolls foaming over a bed of rocks.
The noise of the water frightened Virginia, and she
durst not wade through the stream: Paul therefore took
her up in his arms, and went thus loaded over the
slippery rocks, which formed the bed of the river,
careless of the tumultuous noise of its waters. 'Do not

be afraid,' cried he to Virginia; 'I feel very strong with you. If the inhabitant of the Black River had refused you the pardon of his slave, I would have fought with him.' — 'What!' answered Virginia, 'with that great wicked man? To what have I exposed you! Gracious heaven! How difficult it is to do good! and it is so easy to do wrong.'

"When Paul had crossed the river, he wished to continue his journey, carrying his sister, and believed he was able to climb in that way the mountain of the Three Peaks, which was still at the distance of half a league; but his strength soon failed, and he was obliged to set down his burden, and to rest himself by her side. Virginia then said to him, 'My dear brother the sun is going down: you have still some strength left, but mine has quite failed: do leave me here, and return home alone to ease the fears of our mothers.' — 'Oh, no,' said Paul, 'I will not leave you. If night surprises us in this wood, I will light a fire, and bring down another palm tree: you shall eat the cabbage; and I will form a covering of the leaves to shelter you.' In the meantime, Virginia being a little rested, pulled from the trunk of an old tree, which hung over the bank of the river, some long leaves of hart's tongue, which grew near its root. With those leaves she made a sort of buskin, with which she covered her feet, that were bleeding from the sharpness of the stony paths; for, in her eager desire to do good, she had forgot to put on her shoes. Feeling her feet cooled by the freshness of the leaves, she broke off a branch of bamboo, and continued her walk leaning with one hand on the staff, and with the other on Paul.

"They walked on slowly through the woods, but from the height of the trees, and the thickness of their foliage, they soon lost sight of the mountain of the Tree Peaks, by which they had directed their course, and even of the sun, which was now setting. At length they wandered without perceiving it, from the beaten path in which they had hitherto walked, and found themselves in a labyrinth of trees and rocks, which appeared to have no opening. Paul made Virginia sit down, while he ran backwards and forwards, half frantic, in search of a path which might lead them out of this thick wood; but all his researches were in vain. He climbed to the top of a tree, from whence he hoped at least to discern the mountain of the Three Peaks; but all he could perceive around him were the tops of trees, some of which were gilded by the last beams of the setting sun. Already the shadows of the mountains were spread over the forests in the valleys. The wind ceased, as it usually does, at the evening hour. The most profound silence reigned in those awful solitudes, which was only interrupted by the cry of the stags, who came to repose in that unfrequented spot. Paul, in the hope that some hunter would hear his voice, called out as loud as he was able, 'Come, come to the help of Virginia.' But the echoes of the forests alone answered his call, and repeated again and again, 'Virginia — Virginia.' Paul at length descended from the tree, overcome with fatigue and vexation, and reflected how they might best contrive to pass the night in that desert. But he could find neither a fountain, a palm tree, nor even a branch of dry wood to kindle a fire. He then felt, by experience, the sense of his own weakness, and began to weep. Virginia said to him, 'Do not weep, my dear brother, or I shall die with grief. I am the cause of all your sorrow, and of all that our mothers suffer at this moment. I find we ought to do nothing, not even good, without consulting our parents. Oh, I have been very imprudent!' and she began to shed tears. She then said to Paul, 'Let us pray to God, my dear brother, and he will hear us.'

"Scarcely had they finished their prayer, when they heard the barking of a dog. 'It is the dog of some hunter,' said Paul, 'who comes here at night to lay in wait for the stags.'

"Soon after the dog barked again with more violence. 'Surely,' said Virginia, 'it is Fidele, our own dog; yes, I know his voice. Are we then so near home? at the foot of our own mountain? a moment after Fidele was at their feet, barking, howling, crying, and devouring them with his caresses. Before they had recovered their surprise, they saw Domingo running towards them. At the sight of this good old Negro, who wept with joy, they began to weep too, without being able to utter one word. When Domingo had recovered himself a little, 'Oh, my dear children,' cried he, 'how miserable have you made your mothers! How much were they astonished when they returned from mass, where I went with them, and not finding you! Mary, who was at work at a little distance, could not tell us where you were gone. I ran backwards and forwards about the plantation, not knowing where to look for you. At last I took some of your old clothes, and showing them to Fidele, the poor animal, as if he understood me, immediately began to scent your path; and conducted me, continually wagging his tail, to the Black River. It was there a planter told me that you had brought back a Negro woman, his slave, and that he had granted you her pardon. But what pardon! he showed her to me with her feet chained to a block of wood, and an iron collar with three hooks fastened round her neck.

"'From thence Fidele, still on the scent, led me up the precipice of the Black River, where he again stopped and barked with all his might. This was on the brink of a spring, near a fallen palm tree, and close to a fire which was still smoking. At last he led me to this very spot. We are at the foot of the mountains of the

Three Peaks, and still four leagues from home. Come, eat, and gather strength.' He then presented them with cakes, fruits, and a very large gourd filled with a liquor composed of wine, water, lemon juice sugar, and nutmeg, which their mothers had prepared. Virginia sighed at the recollection of the poor slave, and at the uneasiness which they had given their mothers. She repeated several times, 'Oh, how difficult it is to do good.'

"While she and Paul were taking refreshment, Domingo kindled a fire, and having sought among the rocks for a particular kind of crooked wood, which burns when quite green, throwing out a great blaze, he made a torch, which he lighted, it being already night. But when they prepared to continue their journey, a new difficulty occurred; Paul and Virginia could no longer walk, their feet being violently swelled and inflamed. Domingo knew not whether it were best to leave them, and go in search of help, or remain and pass the night with them on that spot. 'What is become of the time,' said he, 'when I used to carry you both together in my arms? But now you are grown big, and I am grown old.' While he was in this perplexity, a troop of Maroon Negroes appeared at the distance of twenty paces. The chief of the band, approaching Paul and Virginia, said to them, 'Good little white people, do not be afraid. We saw you pass this morning, with a Negro woman of the Black River. You went to ask pardon for her of her wicked master, and we, in return for this, will carry you home upon our shoulders.' He then made a sign, and four of the strongest Negroes immediately formed a sort of litter with the branches of trees and lianas, in which, having seated Paul and Virginia, they placed it upon their shoulders. Domingo marched in front, carrying his lighted torch, and they proceeded amidst the rejoicings of the whole troop, and overwhelmed with their benedictions. Virginia, affected by this scene, said to Paul, with emotion, 'O, my dear brother! God never leaves a good action without reward.'

"It was midnight when they arrived at the foot of the mountain, on the ridges of which several fires were lighted. Scarcely had they begun to ascend, when they heard voices crying out, 'Is it you, my children?' They answered together with the Negroes, 'Yes, it is us;' and soon after perceived their mothers and Mary coming towards them with lighted sticks in their hands. 'Unhappy children!' cried Madame de la Tour, 'from whence do you come? What agonies you have made us suffer!' 'We come, said Virginia, 'from the Black River, where we went to ask pardon for a poor Maroon slave, to whom I gave our breakfast this morning, because she was dying of hunger; and these Maroon Negroes have brought us home.' — Madame de la Tour embraced her daughter without being able to speak; and Virginia, who felt her face wet with her mother's tears, exclaimed, 'You repay me for all the hardships I have suffered.' Margaret, in a transport of delight, pressed Paul in her arms, crying, 'And you also, my dear child! you have done a good action.' When they reached the hut with their children, they gave plenty of food to the Negroes, who returned to their woods, after praying the blessing of heaven might descend on those good white people.

"Every day was to those families a day of tranquility and of happiness. Neither ambition nor envy disturbed their repose. In this island, where, as in all the European colonies, every malignant anecdote is circulated with avidity, their virtues, and even their names, were unknown. Only when a traveler on the road of the Shaddock Grove inquired of any of the inhabitants of the plain, 'Who lives in those two cottages above?' he was always answered, even by those who did not know them, 'They are good people.' Thus the modest violet, concealed beneath the thorny bushes, sheds its fragrance, while itself remains unseen.

"Doing good appeared to those amiable families to be the chief purpose of life. Solitude, far from having blunted their benevolent feelings, or rendered their dispositions morose, had left their hearts open to every tender affection. The contemplation of nature filled their minds with enthusiastic delight. They adored the bounty of that Providence which had enabled them to spread abundance and beauty amidst those barren rocks, and to enjoy those pure and simple pleasures which are ever grateful and ever new. It was, probably, in those dispositions of mind that Madame de la Tour composed the following sonnet.

SONNET
TO SIMPLICITY

Nymph of the desert! on this lonely shore,
Simplicity, thy blessings still are mine,
And all thou canst not give I pleased resign,
For all beside can soothe my soul no more.
I ask no lavish heaps to swell my store,
And purchase pleasures far remote from thine.
Ye joys, for which the race of Europe pine,
Ah! not for me your studied grandeur pour,
Let me where yon tall cliffs are rudely piled,
Where towers the palm amidst the mountain trees,
Where pendant from the steep, with graces wild,
The blue liana floats upon the breeze,

Still haunt those bold recesses, Nature's child,
Where thy majestic charms my spirit seize!

"Paul, at twelve years of age, was stronger and more
intelligent than Europeans are at fifteen, and had em-
bellished the plantations which Domingo had only
cultivated. He had gone with him to the neighboring
woods, and rooted up young plants of lemon trees,
oranges, and tamarinds, the round heads of which are
of so fresh a green, together with date palm trees,
producing fruit filled with a sweet cream, which has
the fine perfume of the orange flower. Those trees,
which were already of a considerable size, he planted
round this little enclosure. He had also sown the seeds
of many trees which the second year bear flowers or
fruits. The agathis, encircled with long clusters of white
flowers, which hang upon it like the crystal pendants
of a luster. The Persian lilac, which lifts high in air its
gay flax-colored branches. The papaw tree, the trunk
of which, without branches, forms a column set round
with green melons, bearing on their heads large leaves
like those of the fig tree.
"The seeds and kernels of the gum tree, terminalia,
mangoes, alligator pears, the guava, the bread tree, and
the narrow-leaved eugenia, were planted with profusion; and the greater number of those trees already
afforded to their young cultivator both shade and fruit.
His industrious hands had diffused the riches of nature
even on the most barren parts of the plantation. Several
kinds of aloes, the common Indian fig, adorned with
yellow flowers, spotted with red, and the thorny five-
angled touch thistle, grew upon the dark summits of
the rocks, and seemed to aim at reaching the long
lianas, which, loaded with blue or crimson flowers,
hung scattered over the steepest part of the mountain.
Those trees were disposed in such a manner that you

could command the whole at one view. He had placed in the middle of this hollow the plants of the lowest growth: behind grew the shrubs; then trees of an ordinary height: above which rose majestically the venerable lofty groves which border the circumference. Thus from its center this extensive enclosure appeared like a verdant amphitheater spread with fruits and flowers, containing a variety of vegetables, a chain of meadow land, and fields of rice and corn. In blending those vegetable productions to his own taste, he followed the designs of Nature. Guided by her suggestions, he had thrown upon the rising grounds such seeds as the winds might scatter over the heights, and near the borders of the springs such grains as float upon the waters. Every plant grew in its proper soil, and every spot seemed decorated by her hands. The waters, which rushed from the summits of the rocks, formed in some parts of the valley limpid fountains, and in other parts were spread into large clear mirrors, which reflected the bright verdure, the trees in blossom, the bending rocks, and the azure heavens.

"Notwithstanding the great irregularity of the ground, most of these plantations were easy of access. We had, indeed, all given him our advice and assistance, in order to accomplish this end. He had formed a path which wound round the valley, and of which various ramifications led from the circumference to the center. He had drawn some advantage from the most rugged spots; and had blended, in harmonious variety, smooth walks with the asperities of the soil, and wild with domestic productions. With that immense quantity of rolling stones which now block up those paths, and which are scattered over most of the ground of this island, he formed here and there pyramids; and at their base he laid earth, and planted the roots of rose bushes, the Barbados flower fence, and

other shrubs which love to climb the rocks. In a short
time those gloomy shapeless pyramids were covered
with verdure, or with the glowing tints of the most
beautiful flowers. The hollow recesses of aged trees,
which bent over the borders of the stream, formed
vaulted caves impenetrable to the sun, and where you
might enjoy coolness during the heats of the day. That
path led to a clump of forest trees, in the center of
which grew a cultivated tree, loaded with fruit. Here
was a field ripe with corn, there an orchard. From that
avenue you had a view of the cottages; from this, of
the inaccessible summit of the mountain. Beneath that
tufted bower of gum trees, interwoven with lianas, no
object could be discerned even at noon, while the point
of the neighboring rock, which projects from the
mountain commanded a few of the whole enclosure,
and of the distant ocean, where sometimes we spied a
vessel coming from Europe, or returning thither. On
this rock the two families assembled in the evening,
and enjoyed, in silence, the freshness of the air, the
fragrance of the flowers, the murmurs of the fountains,
and the last blended harmonies of light and shade.

"Nothing could be more agreeable than the names
which were bestowed upon some of the charming
retreats of this labyrinth. That rock, of which I was
speaking, and from which my approach was discerned
at a considerable distance, was called the Discovery of
Friendship. Paul and Virginia, amidst their sports, had
planted a bamboo on that spot; and whenever they saw
me coming, they hoisted a little white handkerchief,
by way of signal of my approach, as they had seen a
flag hoisted on the neighboring mountain at the sight
of a vessel at sea. The idea struck me of engraving an
inscription upon the stalk of this reed. Whatever pleasure I have felt, during my travels, at the sight of a statue
or monument of antiquity, I have felt still more in

reading of well written inscription. It seems to me as if a human voice issued from the stone and making itself heard through the lapse of ages, addressed man in the midst of a desert, and told him that I was not alone; that other men, on that very spot, have felt, and thought, and suffered like himself. If the inscription belongs to an ancient nation which no longer exists, it leads the soul through infinite space, and inspires the feeling of its immortality, by showing that a thought has survived the ruins of an impire.

"I inscribed then, on the little mast of Paul and Virginia's flag, those lines of Horace:

Fratres Helenae, lucida sidera,
Ventorumque regat pater,
Obstrictis alils, praeter Iapyga.

'May the brothers of Helen, lucid stars like you, and the Father of the winds, guide you; and may you only feel the breath of the zephyr.'

"I engraved this line of Virgil upon the bark of a gum tree, under the shade of which Paul sometimes seated himself, in order to contemplate the agitated sea: —

Fortunatue et ille deos qui novit agrestes!

'Happy art thou, my son, to know only the pastoral divinities.'

"And above the door of Madame de la Tour's cottage, where the families used to assemble, I placed this line:

At secura quies, et nescia fallere vita.

'Here is a calm conscience, and a life ignorant

of deceit.'

"But Virginia did not approve of my Latin; she said, that what I had placed at the foot of her weather flag was too long and too learned. 'I should have liked better,' added she, 'to have seen inscribed, *Always agitated, yet ever constant.*'

"The sensibility of those happy families extended itself to everything around them. They had given names the most tender to objects in appearance the most indifferent. A border of orange, plantain, and bread trees, planted round a greensward where Virginia and Paul sometimes danced, was called Concord. An old tree, beneath the shade of which Madame de la Tour and Margaret used to relate their misfortunes, was called, The Tears wiped away. They gave the names of Brittany and Normandy to little portions of ground where they had sown corn, strawberries, and peas. Domingo and Mary, wishing, in imitation of their mistresses, to recall the places of their birth in Africa, gave the names of Angola and Foullepointe to the spots where grew the herb with which they wove baskets, and where they had planted a calbassia tree. Thus, with the productions of their respective climates, those exiled families cherished the dear illusions which bind us to our native country, and softened their regrets in a foreign land. Alas! I have seen animated by a thousand soothing appellations, those trees, those fountains, those stones which are now overthrown, which now, like the plains of Greece, present nothing but ruins and affecting remembrances.

"Neither the neglect of her European friends, nor the delightful romantic spot which she inhabited, could banish from the mind of Madame de la Tour this tender attachment to her native country. While the luxurious fruits of this climate gratified the taste of her family, she delighted to rear those which were more graceful, only because they were the productions of her early home. Among other little pieces addressed to flowers and fruits of northern climes, I found the following sonnet to the Strawberry.

SONNET
TO THE STRAWBERRY

The strawberry blooms upon its lowly bed:
Plant of my native soil! The lime may fling
More potent fragrance on the zephyr's wing,
The milky cocoa richer juices shed,
The white guava lovelier blossoms spread:
But not, like thee, to fond remembrance bring
The vanish'd hours of life's enchanting spring;
Short calendar of joys forever fled!
Thou bidst the scenes of childhood rise to view,
The wild wood path which fancy loves to trace,
Where, veil'd in leaves, thy fruit of rosy hue,
Lurk'd on its pliant stem with modest grace.
But, ah! when thought would later years renew,
Alas! successive sorrows crowd the space.

"But perhaps the most charming spot of this enclosure was that which was called the Repose of Virginia. At the foot of the rock which bore the name of the Discovery of Friendship, is a nook, from whence issues a fountain, forming, near its source, a little spot of marshy soil in the midst of a field of rich grass. At the time Margaret was delivered of Paul, I made her a present of an Indian cocoa which had been given me, and which she planted on the border of this fenny ground, in order that the tree might one day serve to mark the epocha of her son's birth. Madame de la Tour planted another cocoa, with the same view, at the birth of Virginia. Those fruits produced two cocoa trees, which formed all the records of the two families: one was called the tree of Paul, the other the tree of Virginia. They grew in the same proportion as the two young persons, of an unequal height; but they rose, at the end of twelve years, above the cottages. Already their tender stalks were interwoven, and their young branches of cocoas hung over the basin of the fountain. Except this little plantation, the nook of the rock had been left as it was decorated by nature. On its brown and humid sides large plants of maidenhair glistened with their green and dark stars; and tufts of wave-leaved hartstongue, suspended like long ribbons of purpled green, floated on the winds. Near this grew a chain of the Madagascar periwinkle, the flowers of which resemble the red gillyflower; and the long-podded capsicum, the cloves of which are of the color of blood, and more glowing than coral. The herb of balm, with its leaves within the heart, and the sweet basil, which has the odor of the gillyflower, exhaled the most delicious perfumes. From the steep summit of the mountain hung the graceful lianas, like a floating drapery, forming magnificent canopies of verdure upon the sides of the rocks. The sea birds, allured by the stillness of those retreats, resorted thither to pass the night. At the hour of sunset we perceived the curlew and the stint skimming along the seashore; the cardinal poised high in air; and the white bird of the tropic, which abandons, with the star of day, the solitudes of the Indian ocean. Virginia loved to repose upon the border of this fountain, decorated with wild and sublime magnificence.

She often seated herself beneath the shade of the two cocoa trees, and there she sometimes led her goats to graze. While she prepared cheeses of their milk, she loved to see them browse on the maidenhair which grew upon the steep sides of the rock, and hung suspended upon one of its cornices, as on a pedestal. Paul, observing that Virginia was fond of this spot, brought thither, from the neighboring forest, a great variety of birds' nests. The old birds, following their young, established themselves in this new colony. Virginia, at stated times, distributed amongst them grains of rice, millet, and maize. As soon as she appeared, the whistling blackbird, the amadavid bird, the note of which is so soft: the cardinal, the black frigate bird, with its plumage the color of flame, forsook their bushes; the parakeet, green as an emerald, descended from the neighboring fan palms; the partridge ran along the grass: all advanced promiscuously towards her, like a brood of chickens: and she and Paul delighted to observe their sports, their repasts, and their loves.

"Amiable children! thus passed your early days in innocence, and in the exercise of benevolence. How many times, on this very spot, have your mothers, pressing you in their arms, blessed Heaven for the consolations your unfolding virtues prepared for their declining years, while already they enjoyed the satisfaction of seeing you begin life under the most happy auspices! How many times, beneath the shade of those rocks, have I partaken with them of your rural repasts, which cost no animal its life. Gourds filled with milk, fresh eggs, cakes of rice placed upon plantain leaves, baskets loaded with mangoes, oranges, dates, pomegranates, pine-apples, furnished at the same time the most wholesome food, the most beautiful colors, and the most delicious juices.

"The conversation was gentle and innocent as the

repasts. Paul often talked of the labors of the day, and those of the morrow. He was continually forming some plan of accommodation for their little society. Here he discovered that the paths were rough; there that the family circle was ill seated: sometimes the young arbors did not afford sufficient shade, and Virginia might be better pleased elsewhere.

"In the rainy seasons the two families assembled together in the hut, and employed themselves in weaving mats of grass, and baskets of bamboo. Rakes, spades, and hatchets were ranged along the walls in the most perfect order; and near those instruments of agriculture were placed the productions which were the fruits of labor: sacks of rice, sheaves of corn, and baskets of the plantain fruit. Some degree of luxury is usually united with plenty; and Virginia was taught by her mother and Margaret to prepare sherbet and cordials from the juice of the sugar-cane, the orange, and the citron.

"When night came, those families supped together by the light of a lamp; after which, Madame de la Tour or Margaret related histories of travelers lost during the night in such of the forests of Europe as are infested by banditti; or told a dismal tale of some shipwrecked vessel, thrown by the tempest upon the rocks of a desert island. To these recitals their children listened with eager sensibility, and earnestly begged that Heaven would grant they might one day have the joy of showing their hospitality towards such unfortunate persons. At length the two families separated and retired to rest, impatient to meet again the next morning. Sometimes they were lulled to repose by the beating rains, which fell in torrents upon the roof of their cottages; and sometimes by the hollow winds, which brought to their ear the distant murmur of the waves breaking upon the shore. They blessed God for their personal safety, of which their feeling became stronger from the idea of remote danger.

"Madame de la Tour occasionally read aloud some affecting history of the Old or New Testament. Her auditors reasoned but little upon those sacred books, for their theology consisted in sentiment, like that of nature: and their morality in action, like that of the gospel. Those families had no particular days devoted to pleasure, and others to sadness. Every day was to them a holiday, and all which surrounded them one holy temple, where they forever adored an Infinite Intelligence, the friend of human kind. A sentiment of confidence in his supreme power filled their minds with consolation under the past, with fortitude for the present, and with hope for the future. Thus, compelled by misfortune to return to a state of nature, those women had unfolded in their own bosoms, and in those of their children, the feelings which are most natural to the human mind, and which are our best support under evil.

"But as clouds sometimes arise which cast a gloom over the best regulated tempers, whenever melancholy took possession of any member of this little society, the rest endeavored to banish painful thoughts rather by sentiment than by arguments. Margaret exerted her gaiety; Madame de la Tour employed her mild theology; Virginia, her tender caresses; Paul, his cordial and engaging frankness. Even Mary and Domingo hastened to offer their succor, and to weep with those that wept. Thus weak plants are interwoven, in order to resist the tempests.

"During the fine season they went every Sunday to the church of the Shaddock Grove, the steeple of which you see yonder upon the plain. After service, the poor often came to require some kind office at their hands. Sometimes an unhappy creature sought their advice, sometimes a child led them to its sick mother in the neighborhood. They always took with them remedies for the ordinary diseases of the country, which they administered in that soothing manner which stamps so much value upon the smallest favors. Above all, they succeeded in banishing the disorders of the mind, which are so intolerable in solitude, and under the infirmities of a weakened frame. Madame de la Tour spoke with such sublime confidence of the Divinity, that the sick, while listening to her, believed that he was present. Virginia often returned home with her eyes wet with tears and her heart overflowing with delight, having had an opportunity of doing good. After those visits of charity, they sometimes prolonged their way by the Sloping Mountain, till they reached my dwelling, where I had prepared dinner for them upon the banks of the little river which glides near my cottage. I produced on those occasions some bottles of old wine, in order to heighten the gaiety of our Indian repast by the cordial productions of Europe. Sometimes we met upon the seashore, at the mouth of little rivers, which are here scarcely larger than brooks. We brought from the plantation our vegetable provisions, to which we added such as the sea furnished in great variety. Seated upon a rock, beneath the shade of the velvet sunflower, we heard the mountain billows break at our feet with a dashing noise; and sometimes on that spot we listened to the plaintive strains of the water curlew Madame de la Tour answered his sorrowful notes in the following sonnet: —

SONNET
TO THE CURLEW

Sooth'd by the murmurs on the sea-beat shore
His dun grey plumage floating to the gale,
The curlew blends his melancholy wail
With those hoarse sounds the rushing waters pour.
Like thee, congenial bird: my steps explore
The bleak lone sea beach, or the rocky dale,
And shun the orange bower, the myrtle vale,
Whose gay luxuriance suits my soul no more.
I love the ocean's broad expanse, when dress'd
In limpid clearness, or when tempests blow.
When the smooth currents on its placid breast
Flow calm, as my past moments us'd to flow;
Or when its troubled waves refuse to rest,
And seem the symbol of my present woe.

"Our repasts were succeeded by the songs and dances
of the two young people. Virginia sang the happiness
of pastoral life, and the misery of those who were
impelled, by avarice, to cross the furious ocean, rather
than cultivate the earth, and enjoy its peaceful boun-
ties. Sometimes she performed a pantomime with Paul,
in the manner of the Negroes. The first language of
man is pantomime; it is known to all nations, and is
so natural and so expressive, that the children of the
European inhabitants catch it with facility from the
Negroes. Virginia recalling, amongst the histories
which her mother had read to her, those which had
affected her most, represented the principal events with
beautiful simplicity. Sometimes at the sound of Domingo's tantam she appeared upon the greensward, bear-

ing a pitcher upon her head, and advanced with a timid step towards the source of a neighboring fountain, to draw water. Domingo and Mary, who personated the shepherds of Midian, forbade her to approach, and repulsed her sternly. Upon which Paul flew to her succor, beat away the shepherds, filled Virginia's pitcher, and placing it upon her head, bound her brows at the same time with a wreath of the red flowers of the Madagascar periwinkle, which served to heighten the delicacy of her skin. Then, joining their sports, I took upon me the part of Raguel, and bestowed upon Paul my daughter Zephora in marriage.

"Sometimes Virginia represented the unfortunate Ruth, returning poor and widowed to her own country, where after so long an absence, she found herself as in a foreign land. Domingo and Mary personated the reapers. Virginia followed their steps, gleaning here and there a few ears of corn. She was interrogated by Paul with the gravity of a patriarch, and answered, with a faltering voice, his questions. Soon touched with compassion, he granted an asylum to innocence, and hospitality to misfortune. He filled Virginia's lap with plenty; and, leading her towards us, as before the old men of the city, declared his purpose to take her in marriage. At this scene, Madame de la Tour, recalling the desolate situation in which she had been left by her relations, her widowhood, the kind reception she had met with from Margaret, succeeded by the soothing hope of a happy union between their children, could not forbear weeping; and the sensations which such recollections excited led the whole audience to pour forth those luxurious tears which have their mingled source in sorrow and in joy.

"These dramas were performed with such an air of reality, that you might have fancied yourself transported to the plains of Syria or of Palestine. We were not unfurnished, with either decorations, lights, or an orchestra, suitable to the representation. The scene was generally placed in an opening of the forest, where such parts of the wood as were penetrable formed around us numerous arcades of foliage, beneath which we were sheltered from the heat during the whole day; but when the sun descended towards the horizon, its rays, broken upon the trunks of the trees, diverged amongst the shadows of the forest in strong lines of light, which produced the most sublime effect. Sometimes the whole of its broad disk appeared at the end of an avenue, spreading one dazzling mass of brightness. The foliage of the trees, illuminated from beneath by its saffron beams, glowed with the luster of the topaz and the emerald. Their brown and mossy trunks appeared transformed into columns of antique bronze; and the birds, which had retired in silence to their leafy shades to pass the night, surprised to see the radiance of a second morning, hailed the star of day with innumerable carols.

"Night soon overtook us during those rural entertainments; but the purity of the air, and the mildness of the climate, admitted of our sleeping in the woods secure from the injuries of the weather, and no less secure from the molestation of robbers. At our return the following day to our respective habitations, we found them exactly in the same state in which they had been left. In this island, which then had no commerce, there was so much simplicity and good faith, that the doors of several houses were without a key, and a lock was an object of curiosity to many of the natives.

"Amidst the luxuriant beauty of this favored climate, Madame de la Tour often regretted the quick succession from day to night which takes place between the tropics, and which deprived her pensive mind of that hour of twilight, the softened gloom of which is so soothing and sacred to the feelings of tender melancholy. This regret is expressed in the following sonnet: —

SONNET
TO THE TORRID ZONE

Pathway of light! o'er thy empurpled zone
With lavish charms perennial summer strays;
Soft 'midst thy spicy groves the zephyr plays,
While far around the rich perfumes are thrown:
The amadavid bird for thee alone
Spreads his gay plumes, that catch thy vivid rays,
For thee the gems with liquid luster blaze,
And Nature's various wealth is all thy own.
But, ah! not thine is twilight's doubtful gloom,
Those mild gradations, mingling day with night;
Here instant darkness shrouds thy genial bloom,
Nor leaves my pensive soul that lingering light,
When musing memory would each trace resume
Of fading pleasures in successive flight.

"Paul and Virginia had neither clock nor almanac, nor books of chronology, history, or philosophy. The periods of their lives were regulated by those of nature. They knew the hours of the day by the shadows of the trees, the seasons by the times when those trees bore flowers or fruit, and the years by the number of their harvests. These soothing images diffused an inexpressible charm over their conversation. 'It is time to dine,' said Virginia, 'the shadows of the plantain trees are at their roots; or, 'night approaches; the tamarinds close their leaves.' 'When will you come to see us?' inquired some of her companions in the neighborhood. 'At the time of the sugar canes,' answered Virginia. 'Your visit will be then still more delightful,' resumed her young acquaintances. When she was asked what was her own age, and that of Paul, 'My brother,' said she, 'is as old as the great cocoa tree of the fountain; and I am as old as the little cocoa tree. The mangoes have borne fruit twelve times, and the orange trees have borne flowers four-and-twenty times, since I came into the world.' Their lives seemed linked to the trees like those of fauns or dryads. They knew no other historical epochas than that of the lives of their mothers, no other chronology than that of their orchards, and no other philosophy than that of doing good, and resigning themselves to the will of Heaven.

"Thus grew those children of nature. No care had troubled their peace, no intemperance had corrupted their blood, no misplaced passion had depraved their hearts. Love, innocence, and piety, possessed their souls; and those intellectual graces unfolded themselves in their features, their attitudes, and their motions. Still in the morning of life, they had all its blooming freshness; and surely such in the garden of Eden appeared our first parents, when, coming from the hands of God, they first saw, approached, and conversed together, like brother and sister. Virginia was gentle, modest, and confiding as Eve; and Paul, like Adam, united the figure of manhood with the simplicity of a child.

"When alone with Virginia, he has a thousand times told me, he used to say to her, at his return from labor, 'When I am wearied, the sight of you refreshes me. If from the summit of the mountain I perceive you below in the valley, you appear to me in the midst of our orchard like a blushing rosebud. If you go towards our mother's house, the partridge, when it runs to meet its young has a shape less beautiful, and a step less light. When I lose sight of you through the trees, I have no need to see you in order to find you again. Something of you, I know not how, remains for me in the air where you have passed, in the grass where you have been seated. When I come near you, you delight all my senses. The azure of heaven is less charming than the blue of your eyes, and the song of the amadavid bird less soft than the sound of your voice. If I only touch you with my finger, my whole frame trembles with pleasure. Do you remember the day when we crossed over the great stones of the river of the Three Peaks; I was very much tired before we reached the bank; but as soon as I had taken you in my arms, I seemed to have wings like a bird. Tell me by what charm you have so enchanted me? Is it by your wisdom? Our mothers have more than either of us. Is it by your caresses? They embrace me much oftener than you. I think it must be by your goodness. I shall never forget how you walked barefooted to the Black River, to ask pardon for the poor wandering; slave. Here, my beloved, take this flowering orange branch, which I have culled in the forest; you will place it at night near your bed. Eat this honeycomb, which I have taken for you from the top of a rock. But first lean upon my bosom, and I shall be refreshed.'

"Virginia then answered, 'Oh my dear brother, the rays of the sun in the morning at the top of the rocks give me less joy than the sight of you. I love my mother, I love yours; but when they call you their son, I love them a thousand times more. When they caress you, I feel it more sensibly than when I am caressed myself. You ask me why you love me. Why, all creatures that are brought up together love one another. Look at our birds reared up in the same nests; they love like us; they are always together like us. Hark? how they call and answer from one tree to another. So when the echoes bring to my ears the air which you play upon your flute at the top of the mountain, I repeat the words at the bottom of the valley. Above all, you are dear to me since the day when you wanted to fight the master of the slave for me. Since that time how often have I said to myself, 'Ah, my brother has a good heart; but for him I should have died of terror.' I pray to God every day for my mother and yours; for you, and for our poor servants; but when I pronounce your name, my devotion seems to increase, I ask so earnestly of God that no harm may befall you! Why do you go so far, and climb so high, to seek fruits and flowers for me? How much you are fatigued!' and with her little white handkerchief she wiped the damps from his brow.

"For some time past, however, Virginia had felt her heart agitated by new sensations. Her fine blue eyes lost their luster, her cheek its freshness, and her frame was seized with universal languor. Serenity no longer sat upon her brow, nor smiles played upon her lips. She became suddenly gay without joy, and melancholy without vexation. She fled her innocent sports, her gentle labors, and the society of her beloved family; wandering along the most unfrequented parts of the plantation, and seeking everywhere that rest which she could no where find. Sometimes, at the sight of Paul, she advanced sportively towards him, and, when going to accost him, was seized with sudden confusion: her pale cheeks were overspread with blushes, and her eyes no longer dared to meet those of her brother. Paul said to her, 'The rocks are covered with verdure, our birds begin to sing when you approach, everything around you is gay, and you only are unhappy.' He endeavored to soothe her by his embraces; but she turned away her head, and fled trembling towards her mother. The caresses of her brother excited too much emotion in her agitated heart. Paul could not comprehend the meaning of those new and strange caprices.

"One of those summers, which sometimes desolate the countries situated between the tropics, now spread its ravages over this island. It was near the end of December, when the sun in Capricorn darts over Mauritius, during the space of three weeks, its vertical fires. The south wind, which prevails almost throughout the whole year, no longer blew. Vast columns of dust arose from the highways, and hung suspended in the air: the ground was everywhere broken into clefts; the grass was burned; hot exhalations issued from the sides of the mountains, and their rivulets, for the most part became dry: fiery vapors, during the day, ascended from the plains, and appeared, at the setting of the sun, like a conflagration. Night brought no coolness to the heated atmosphere: the orb of the moon seemed of blood, and, rising in a misty horizon, appeared of supernatural magnitude. The drooping cattle, on the sides of the hills, stretching out their necks towards heaven, and panting for air, made the valleys reecho with their melancholy lowings; even the Caffree, by whom they were led, threw himself upon the earth, in search of coolness; but the scorching sun had everywhere penetrated, and the stifling atmosphere resounded with the buzzing noise of insects, who sought to allay their thirst in the blood of man and of animals.

"On one of those sultry nights Virginia, restless and unhappy, arose, then went again to rest, but could find in no attitude either slumber or repose. At length she bent her way, by the light of the moon, towards her fountain, and gazed at its spring, which, notwithstanding the drought, still flowed like silver threads down the brown sides of the rock. She flung herself into the basin; its coolness reanimated her spirits, and a thousand soothing remembrances presented themselves to her mind. She recollected that in her infancy her mother and Margaret amused themselves by bathing her with Paul in this very spot; that Paul afterwards, reserving this bath for her use only, had dug its bed, covered the bottom with sand, and sown aromatic herbs around the borders. She saw, reflected through the water upon her naked arms and bosom, the two cocoa trees which were planted at her birth and that of her brother, and which interwove about her head their green branches and young fruit. She thought of Paul's friendship, sweeter than the odors, purer than the waters of the fountains, stronger than the intertwining palm trees, and she sighed. Reflecting upon the hour of the night, and the profound solitude, her imagination again grew disordered. Suddenly she flew affrighted from those dangerous shades, and those waters which she fancied hotter than the torrid sunbeam, and ran to her mother, in order to find a refuge from herself. Often, wishing to unfold her sufferings, she pressed her mother's hand within her own; often she was ready to pronounce the name of Paul; but her oppressed heart left not her lips the power of utterance; and, leaning her head on her mother's bosom, she could only bathe it with her tears.

"Madame de la Tour, though she easily discerned the source of her daughter's uneasiness, did not think proper to speak to her on that subject. 'My dear child,' said she, address yourself to God, who disposes, at his will, of health and of life. He tries you now, in order to recompense you hereafter. Remember that we are only placed upon earth for the exercise of virtue.'

"The excessive heat drew vapors from the ocean, which hung over the island like a vast awning, and slithered round the summits of the mountains, while long flakes of fire occasionally issued from their misty peaks. Soon after the most terrible thunder reechoed through the woods, the plains and the valleys; the rains fell from the skies like cataracts; foaming torrents rolled down the sides of the mountain; the bottom of the valley became a sea; the plat of ground on which the cottages were built, a little island: and the entrance of this valley a sluice, along which rushed precipitately the moaning waters, earth, trees, and rocks.

"Meantime the trembling family addressed their prayers to God in the cottage of Madame de la Tour, the roof of which cracked horribly from the struggling winds. So vivid and frequent were the lightnings, that, although the doors and window-shutters were well fastened, every object without was distinctly seen through the jointed beams. Paul, followed by Domingo, went with intrepidity from one cottage to another, notwithstanding the fury of the tempest; here supporting a partition with a buttress, there driving in a stake, and only returning to the family to calm their fears, by the hope that the storm was passing away. Accordingly, in the evening the rains ceased, the trade-winds of the south pursued their ordinary course, the tempestuous clouds were thrown towards the north-east, and the setting sun appeared in the horizon.

"Virginia's first wish was to visit the spot called her *Repose.* Paul approached her with a timid air, and offered her the assistance of his arm, which she accepted, smiling, and they left the cottage together. The air was fresh and clear; white vapors arose from the ridges of the mountains, furrowed here and there by the foam of the torrents, which were now becoming dry. The garden was altogether destroyed by the hollows which the floods had worn, the roots of the fruit trees were for the most part laid bare, and vast heaps of sand covered the chain of meadows, and choked up Virginia's bath. The two cocoa trees, however, were still erect, and still retained their freshness: but they were no longer surrounded by turf, or arbors, or birds, except a few amadavid birds, who, upon the points of the neighboring rocks, lamented, in plaintive notes, the loss of their young.

"At the sight of this general desolation, Virginia exclaimed to Paul, 'You brought birds hither, and the hurricane has killed them. You planted this garden, and it is now destroyed. Everything then upon earth perishes, and it is only heaven that is not subject to change.' 'Why,' answered Paul, 'why cannot I give you something which belongs to heaven? but I am possessed of nothing even upon earth.' Virginia, blushing, resumed, 'You have the picture of Saint Paul.' Scarcely had she pronounced the words, when he flew in search of it to his mother's cottage. This picture was a small miniature, representing Paul the Hermit, and which Margaret, who was very pious, had long worn hung at her neck when she was a girl, and which, since she became a mother, she had placed round the neck of her child. It had even happened, that being while pregnant, abandoned by the whole world, and continually employed in contemplating the image of this benevolent recluse, her offspring had contracted, at least so she fancied, some resemblance to this revered object. She therefore bestowed upon him the name of Paul, giving him for his patron a saint, who had passed his life far from mankind, by whom he had been first deceived, and then forsaken. Virginia, upon receiving this little picture from the hands of Paul, said to him, with emotion, 'My dear brother, I will never part with this while I live; nor will I ever forget that you have given me the only thing which you possess in the world.' At this tone of friendship this unhoped-for return of familiarity and tenderness, Paul attempted to embrace her; but, light as a bird, she fled, and left him astonished, and unable to account for a conduct so extraordinary.

"Meanwhile Margaret said to Madame de la Tour, 'Why do we not unite our children by marriage? They have a tender attachment to each other.' Madame de la Tour replied, 'They are too young, and too poor. What grief would it occasion us to see Virginia bring into the world unfortunate children, whom she would not perhaps have sufficient strength to rear! Your Negro, Domingo, is almost too old to labor; Mary is infirm. As for myself, my dear friend, in the space of fifteen years I find my strength much failed; age advances rapidly in hot climates, and, above all, under the pressure of misfortune. Paul is our only hope: let us wait till his constitution is strengthened, and till he can support us by his labor: at present you well know that we have only sufficient to supply the wants of the day: but were we to send Paul for a short time to the Indies, commerce would furnish him with the means of purchasing a slave; and at his return we will unite him to Virginia: for I am persuaded no one on earth can render her so happy as your son. We will consult our neighbor on this subject.

"They accordingly asked my advice, and I was of their opinion. 'The Indian seas,' I observed to them, are calm, and, in choosing a favorable season, the voyage is seldom longer than six weeks. We will furnish Paul with a little venture in my neighborhood, where he is much beloved. If we were only to supply him with some raw cotton, of which we make no use, for want of mills to work it, some ebony, which is here so common, that it serves us for firing, and some resin, which is found in our woods: all those articles will sell advantageously in the Indies, though to us they are useless.'

"I engaged to obtain permission from Monsieur de

la Bourdonnais to undertake this voyage: but I determined previously to mention the affair to Paul; and
my surprise was great, when this young man said to
me, with a degree of good sense above his age, 'And
why do you wish me to leave my family for this
precarious pursuit of fortune? Is there any commerce
more advantageous than the culture of the ground,
which yields sometimes fifty or a hundred fold? If we
wish to engage in commerce, we can do so by carrying
our superfluities to the town, without my wandering
to the Indies. Our mothers tell me, that Domingo is
old and feeble; but I am young, and gather strength
every day. If any accident should happen during my
absence, above all, to Virginia, who already suffers —
Oh, no, no! — I cannot resolve to learn them.'

"This answer threw me into great perplexity, for
Madame de la Tour had not concealed from me the
situation of Virginia, and her desire of separating those
young people for a few years. These ideas I did not dare
to suggest to Paul.

"At this period, a ship, which arrived from France,
brought Madame de la Tour a letter from her aunt.
Alarmed by the terrors of approaching death, which
could alone penetrate a heart so insensible, recovering
from a dangerous disorder, which had left her in a state
of weakness, rendered incurable by age, she desired that
her niece would return to France; or, if her health
forbade her to undertake so long a voyage, she conjured her to send Virginia, on whom she would bestow
a good education, procure for her a splendid marriage,
and leave her the inheritance of her whole fortune. The
perusal of this letter spread general consternation
through the family. Domingo and Mary began to
weep. Paul, motionless with surprise, appeared as if his
heart was ready to burst with indignation; while Virginia, fixing her eyes upon her mother, had not power

to utter a word.

"'And can you now leave us?' cried Margaret to Madame de la Tour. 'No, my dear friend, no, my beloved children,' replied Madame de la Tour; 'I will not leave you. I have lived with you, and with you I will die. I have known no happiness but in your affection. If my health be deranged, my past misfortunes are the cause. My heart, deeply wounded by the cruelty of a relation, and the loss of my husband, has found more consolation and felicity with you beneath these humble huts, than all the wealth of my family could now give me in my own country.'

"At this soothing language every eye overflowed with tears of delight. Paul pressed Madame de la Tour in his arms, exclaiming, 'Neither will I leave you! I will not go to the Indies. We will all labor for you, my dear mother; and you shall never feel any wants with us.' But of the whole society, the person who displayed the least transport, and who probably felt the most, was Virginia; and, during the remainder of the day, that gentle gaiety which flowed from her heart, and proved that her peace was restored, completed the general satisfaction.

"The next day, at sunrise, while they were offering up, as usual, their morning sacrifice of praise, which preceded their breakfast, Domingo informed them that a gentleman on horseback, followed by two slaves, was coming towards the plantation. This person was Monsieur de la Bourdonnais. He entered the cottage where he found the family at breakfast. Virginia had prepared, according to the custom of the country, coffee and rice boiled in water: to which she added hot yams and fresh cocoas. The leaves of the plantain tree supplied the want of table-linen; and calbassia shells, split in two, served for utensils. The governor expressed some surprise at the homeliness of the dwelling: then, addressing himself to Madame de la Tour, he observed, that although public affairs drew his attention too much from the concerns of individuals, she had many claims to his good offices. 'You have an aunt at Paris, Madam,' he added, 'a woman of quality, and immensely rich, who expects that you will hasten to see her, and who means to bestow upon you her whole fortune.' Madame de la Tour replied, that the state of her health would not permit her to undertake so long a voyage. 'At least,' resumed Monsieur de la Bourdonnais, 'you cannot, without injustice, deprive this amiable young lady, your daughter, of so noble an inheritance. I will not conceal from you that your aunt has made use of her influence to oblige you to return; and that I have received official letters, in which I am ordered to exert my authority, if necessary, to that effect. But, as I only wish to employ my power for the purpose of rendering the inhabitants of this colony happy, I expect from your good sense the voluntary sacrifice of a few years, upon which depend your daughter's establishment in the world, and the welfare of your whole life. Wherefore do we come to these islands? Is it not to acquire a fortune? And will it not be more agreeable to return and find it in your own country?'

"He then placed a great bag of piastres, which had been brought hither by one of his slaves, upon the table. 'This,' added he, 'is allotted by your aunt for the preparations necessary for the young lady's voyage.' Gently reproaching Madame de la Tour for not having had recourse to him in her difficulties, he extolled at the same time her noble fortitude. Upon this, Paul said to the governor, 'My mother did, address herself to you, Sir, and you received her ill.' — 'Have you another child, Madam? said Monsieur de la Bourdonnais to Madame de la Tour. — 'No, Sir,' she replied: 'this is the child of my friend; but he and Virginia are equally dear to us.' 'Young man,' said the governor to Paul, 'when you have acquired a little more experience of the world, you will know that it is the misfortune of people in place to be deceived and thence to bestow upon intriguing vice that which belongs to modest merit.'

"Monsieur de la Bourdonnais, at the request of Madame de la Tour, placed himself next her at the table, and breakfasted in the manner of the Creoles, upon coffee mixed with rice boiled in water. He was delighted with the order and neatness which prevailed in the little cottage, the harmony of the two interesting families, and the zeal of their old servants. 'Here,' exclaimed he, 'I discern only wooden furniture, but I find serene contenances, and hearts of gold.' Paul, enchanted with the affability of the governor, said to him, 'I wish to be your friend; you are a good man.' Monsieur de la Bourdonnais received with pleasure this insular compliment, and, taking Paul by the hand, assured him that he might rely upon his friendship.

"After breakfast, he took Madame de la Tour aside, and informed her that an opportunity presented itself of sending her daughter to France in a ship which was going to sail in a short time; that he would recommend her to a lady a relation of his own, who would be a passenger; and that she must not think of renouncing an immense fortune on account of bring separated from her daughter a few years. 'Your aunt,' he added, 'cannot live more than two years; of this I am assured by her friends. Think of it seriously. Fortune does not visit us every day. Consult your friends. Every person of good sense will be of my opinion.' She answered, 'that, desiring no other happiness henceforth in the world than that of her daughter, she would leave her departure for France entirely to her own inclination.

"Madame de la Tour was not sorry to find an opportunity of separating Paul and Virginia for a short time, and provide, by this means, for their mutual felicity at a future period. She took her daughter aside, and said to her, 'My dear child, our servants are now old. Paul is still very young; Margaret is advanced in years, and I am already infirm. If I should die, what will become of you, without fortune, in the midst of these deserts? You will then be left alone without any person who can afford you much succor, and forced to labor without ceasing, in order to support your wretched existence. This idea fills my soul with sorrow.' Virginia answered, 'God has appointed us to labor. You have taught me to labor, and to bless him every day. He never has forsaken us, he never will forsake us. His providence peculiarly watches the unfortunate. You have told me this often my dear mother! I cannot resolve to leave you.' Madame de la Tour replied, with much emotion, 'I have no other aim than to render you happy, and to marry you one day to Paul, who is not your brother. Reflect at present that his fortune depends upon you.'

"A young girl who loves believes that all the world is ignorant of her passion; she throws over her eyes the veil which she has thrown over her heart; but when it is lifted up by some cherishing hand, the secret inquietudes of passion suddenly burst their bounds, and the soothing overflowings of confidence succeed that reserve and mystery with which the oppressed heart had enveloped its feelings. Virginia, deeply affected by this new proof of her mother's tenderness, related to her how cruel had been those struggles which Heaven alone had witnessed; declared that she saw the succor of Providence in that of an affectionate mother, who approved of her attachment, and would guide her by her counsels; that, being now strengthened by such support, every consideration led her to remain with her mother, without anxiety for the present, and without apprehensions for the future.

"Madame de la Tour, perceiving that this confidential conversation had produced an effect altogether different from that which she expected, said, 'My dear child, I will not anymore constrain your inclination: deliberate at leisure, but conceal your feelings from Paul.'

"Towards evening, when Madame de la Tour and Virginia were again together, their confessor, who was a missionary in the island, entered the room, having been sent by the governor. 'My children,' he exclaimed, as he entered, 'God be praised!' you are now rich. You can now listen to the kind suggestion of your excellent hearts, and do good to the poor. I know what Monsieur de la Bourdonnais has said to you, and what you have answered. Your health, dear Madam, obliges you to remain here: but you, young lady, are without excuse. We must obey the will of Providence; and we must also obey our aged relations, even when they are unjust. A sacrifice is required of you; but it is the order of God. He devoted himself for you: and you, in imitation of his example, must devote yourself for the welfare of your family. Your voyage to France will have a happy termination. You will surely consent to go, my dear young lady.'

"Virginia, with downcast eyes, answered, trembling, 'If it be the command of God, I will not presume to oppose it. Let the will of God be done!' said she, weeping.

"The priest went away, and informed the governor of the success of his mission. In the meantime Madame de la Tour sent Domingo to desire I would come hither, that she might consult me upon Virginia's departure. I was of opinion that she ought not to go. I consider it as a fixed principle of happiness, that we ought to prefer the advantages of nature to those of fortune; and never go in search of that at a distance, which we may find in our own bosoms. But what could be expected from my moderate counsels, opposed to the illusions of a splendid fortune; and my simple reasoning, contradicted by the prejudices of the world, and an authority which Madame de la Tour held sacred? This lady had only consulted me from a sentiment of respect, and had, in reality, ceased to deliberate since she had heard the decision of her confessor. Margaret herself, who, notwithstanding the advantages she hoped for her son, from the possession of Virginia's fortune, had hitherto opposed her departure, made no further objections. As for Paul, ignorant of what was decided, and alarmed at the secret conversation which Madame de la Tour held with her daughter, he abandoned himself to deep melancholy. 'They are plotting something against my peace,' cried he, 'since they are so careful of concealment.'

"A report having in the meantime been spread over the island, that fortune had visited those rocks, we beheld merchants of all kinds climbing their steep ascent, and displaying in those humble huts the richest stuffs of India. The fine dimity of Gondelore; the handkerchiefs of Pellicate and Mussulapatan; the plain, striped, and embroidered muslins of Decca, clear as the day. Those merchants unrolled the gorgeous silks of China, white satin damasks, others of grass-green, and bright red; rose-colored taffetas, a profusion of satins, pelongs, and gauze of Tonquin, some plain, and some beautifully decorated with flowers; the soft pekins, downy like cloth; white and yellow nankeens, and the calicoes of Madagascar.

"Madame de la Tour wished her daughter to purchase everything she liked; and Virginia made choice of whatever she believed would be agreeable to her mother, Margaret, and her son. 'This,' said she, 'will serve for furniture, and that will be useful to Mary and Domingo.' In short, the bag of piastres was emptied before she had considered her own wants; and she was obliged to receive a share of the presents which she had distributed to the family circle.

"Paul, penetrated with sorrow at the sight of those gifts of fortune, which he felt were the presage of Virginia's departure, came a few days after to my dwelling. With an air of despondency he said to me, 'My sister is going; they are already making preparations for her voyage. I conjure you to come and exert your influence over her mother and mine, in order to detain her here.' I could not refuse the young man's solicitations, although well convinced that my representations would be unavailing.

"If Virginia had appeared to me charming when clad in the blue cloth of Bengal, with a red handkerchief tied round her head, how much was her beauty improved, when decorated with the graceful ornaments worn by the ladies of this country! She was dressed in white muslin, lined with rose-colored taffeta. Her small and elegant shape was displayed to advantage by her corset, and the lavish profusion of her light tresses were carelessly blended with her simple headdress. Her fine blue eyes were filled with an expression of melancholy: and the struggles of passion, with which her heart was agitated, flushed her cheek, and gave her voice a tone of emotion. The contrast between her pensive look and her gay habiliments rendered her more interesting than ever, nor was it possible to see or hear her unmoved. Paul became more and more melancholy; at length Margaret, distressed by the situation of her son, took him aside, and said to him, 'Why, my dear son, will you cherish vain hopes, which will only render your disappointment more bitter! It is time that I should make known to you the secret of your life and of mine. Mademoiselle de la Tour belongs, by her mother, to a rich and noble family, while you are but the son of a poor peasant girl; and, what is worse, you are a natural child.'

"Paul, who had never before heard this last expression, inquired with eagerness its meaning. His mother replied, 'You had no legitimate father. When I was a girl, seduced by love, I was guilty of a weakness of which you are the offspring. My fault deprived you of the protection of a father's family, and my flight from home, of that of a mother's family. Unfortunate child! you have no relation in the world but me!' And she shed a flood of tears. Paul, pressing her in his arms, exclaimed, 'Oh, my dear mother! since I have no relation in the world but you, I will love you still more! But what a secret have you disclosed to me! I now see the reason why Mademoiselle de la Tour has estranged herself from me for two months past, and why she has determined to go. Ah! I perceive too well that she despises me!'

"'The hour of supper being arrived, we placed ourselves at table; but the different sensations with which we were all agitated left us little inclination to eat, and the meal passed in silence. Virginia first went out, and seated herself on the very spot where we now are placed. Paul hastened after her, and seated himself by her side. It was one of those delicious nights which are so common between the tropics, and the beauty of which no pencil can trace. The moon appeared in the midst of the firmament, curtained in clouds which her beams gradually dispelled. Her light insensibly spread itself over the mountains of the island, and their peaks glistened with a silvered green. The winds were perfectly still. We heard along the woods, at the bottom of the valleys, and on the summits of the rocks, the weak cry and the soft murmurs of the birds, exulting in the brightness of the night, and the serenity of the atmosphere. The hum of insects was heard in the grass. The stars sparkled in the heavens, and their trembling and lucid orbs were reflected upon the bosom of the ocean. Virginia's eyes wandered over its vast and gloomy horizon, distinguishable from the bay of the island by the red fires in the fishing boat. She perceived at the entrance of the harbor a light and a shadow: these were the watch-light and the body of the vessel in which she was to embark for Europe, and which, ready to set sail, lay at anchor, waiting for the wind. Affected at this sight, she turned away her head, in order to hide her tears from Paul.

"Madame de la Tour, Margaret, and myself were seated at a little distance beneath the plantain trees; and amidst the stillness of the night we distinctly heard their conversation, which I have not forgotten.

"Paul said to her, 'You are going, they tell me, in three days. You do not fear, then, to encounter the danger of the sea, at which you are so much terrified!' 'I must fulfill my duty,' answered Virginia, 'by obeying my parent.' 'You leave us,' resumed Paul, 'for a distant relation, whom you have never seen.' 'Alas!' cried Virginia, 'I would have remained my whole life here, but my mother would not have it so. My confessor told me that it was the will of God I should go, and that life was a trial!'

"'What,' exclaimed Paul, 'you have found so many reasons then for going, and not one for remaining here! Ah! there is one reason for your departure, which you have not mentioned. Riches have great attractions. You will soon find in the new world, to which you are going, another to whom you will give the name of brother, which you will bestow on me no more. You will choose that brother from amongst persons who are worthy of you by their birth, and by a fortune which I have not to offer. But where will you go in order to be happier? On what shore will you land which will be dearer to you than the spot which gave you birth? Where will you find a society more interesting to you than this by which you are so beloved? How will you bear to live without your mother's caresses, to which you are so accustomed? What will become of her, already advanced in years, when she will no longer see you at her side at table, in the house, in the walks where she used to lean upon you? What will become of my mother who loves you with the same affection? What shall I say to comfort them when I see them weeping for your absence! Cruel! I speak not to you of myself; but what will become of me, when in the morning I shall no more see you: when the evening will come and will not reunite us? When I shall gaze on the two palm trees, planted at our birth, and so long the witnesses of our mutual friendship? Ah; since a new destiny attracts you, since you seek in a country, distant from your own, other possessions than those which were the fruits of my labor, let me accompany you in the vessel in which you are going to embark. I will animate your courage in the midst of those tempests at which you are so terrified even on shore. I will lay your head on my bosom. I will warm your heart upon my own; and in France, where you go in search of fortune and of grandeur, I will attend you as your slave. Happy only in your happiness, you will find me in those palaces where I shall see you cherished and adored, at least sufficiently noble to make for you the greatest of all sacrifices, by dying at your feet.'

"The violence of his emotion stifled his voice, and we then heard that of Virginia, which, broken by sobs, uttered these words: 'It is for you I go: for you, whom I see every day bent beneath the labor of sustaining two infirm families. If I have accepted this opportunity of becoming rich, it is only to return you a thousand-fold the good which you have done us. Is there any fortune worthy of your friendship? Why do you talk to me of your birth? Ah! if it were again possible to give me a brother, should I make choice of any other than you? Oh, Paul! Paul! you are far dearer to me than a brother! How much has it cost me to avoid you! Help me to tear myself from what I value more than existence, till Heaven can bless our union. But I will stay or go: I will live or die; dispose of me as you will. Unhappy, that I am! I could resist your caresses, but I am unable to support your affliction.'

"At these words Paul seized her in his arms, and, holding her pressed fast to his bosom, cried, in a piercing tone, 'I will go with her; nothing shall divide us.' We ran towards him, and Madame de la Tour said to him, 'My son, if you go, what will become of us?'

"He, trembling, repeated the words, 'My son: — My son' — You my mother,' cried he; 'you, who would separate the brother from the sister! We have both been nourished at your bosom; we have both been reared upon your knees; we have learnt of you to love each other; we have said so a thousand times; and now you would separate her from me! You send her to Europe, that barbarous country which refused you an asylum, and to relations by whom you were abandoned. You will tell me that I have no right over her, and that she is not my sister. She is everything to me, riches, birth, family, my sole good; I know no other. We have had but one roof, one cradle, and we will have but one grave. If she goes, I will follow her. The governor will prevent me! Will he prevent me from flinging myself into the sea? Will he prevent me from following her by swimming? The sea cannot be more fatal to me than the land. Since I cannot live with her, at least I will die before her eyes; far from you, inhuman mother! woman without compassion! May the ocean, to which you trust her, restore her to you no more! May the waves, rolling back our corpses amidst the stones of the beach, give you, in the loss of your two children, an eternal subject of remorse!'

"At these words I seized him in my arms, for despair had deprived him of reason. His eyes flashed fire, big drops of sweat hung upon his face, his knees trembled, and I felt his heart beat violently against his burning bosom.

"Virginia, affrighted, said to him, 'Oh, my friend, I call to witness the pleasures of our early age, your sorrow and my own, and everything that can forever bind two unfortunate beings to each other, that if I remain, I will live but for you; that if I go, I will one day return to be yours. I call you all to witness, you who have reared my infancy, who dispose of my life, who see my tears. I swear by that Heaven which hears me, by the sea which I am going to pass, by the air I breathe, and which I never sullied by a falsehood.'

"As the sun softens and dissolves an icy rock upon the summit of the Apennines, so the impetuous passions of the young man were subdued by the voice of her he loved. He bent his head, and a flood of tears fell from his eyes. His mother, mingling her tears with his, held him in her arms, but was unable to speak. Madame de la Tour, half distracted, said to me, 'I can bear this no longer. My heart is broken. This unfortunate Voyage shall not take place. Do take my son home with you. It is eight days since anyone here has slept.'

"I said to Paul, 'My dear friend, your sister will remain. Tomorrow we will speak to the governor; leave your family, to take some rest, and come and pass the night with me.'

"He suffered himself to be led away in silence; and,

after a night of great agitation, he arose at break of day, and returned home.

"But why should I continue any longer the recital of this history? There is never but one aspect of human life which we can contemplate with pleasure. Like the globe upon which we revolve, our fleeting course is but a day: and if one part of that day be visited by light, the other is thrown into darkness."

"Father," I answered, "finish, I conjure you, the history which you have begun in a manner so interesting. If the images of happiness are most pleasing, those of misfortune are more instructive. Tell me what became of the unhappy young man."

"The first object which Paul beheld in his way home was Mary, who, mounted upon a rock, was earnestly looking towards the sea. As soon as he perceived her, he called to her from a distance, 'Where is Virginia?' Mary turned her head towards her young master, and began to weep. Paul, distracted, and treading back his steps, ran to the harbor. He was there informed, that Virginia had embarked at break of day, that the vessel had immediately after set sail, and could no longer be discerned. He instantly returned to the plantation, which he crossed without uttering a word.

"Although the pile of rocks behind us appears almost perpendicular, those green platforms which separate their summits are so many stages by means of which you may reach, through some difficult paths, that cone of hanging and inaccessible rocks, called the Thumb. At the foot of that cone is a stretching slope of ground, covered with lofty trees, and which is so high and steep that it appears like a forest in air, surrounded by tremendous precipices. The clouds, which are attracted round the summit of those rocks, supply innumerable rivulets, which rush from so immense a height into that deep valley situated behind the mountain, that from this elevated point we do not hear the sound of their fall. On that spot you can discern a considerable part of the island with its precipices crowned with their majestic peaks; and, amongst others, Peterbath, and the three Peaks, with their valley filled with woods. You also command an extensive view of the ocean, and even perceive the Isle of Bourbon forty leagues towards the west. From the summit of that stupendous pile of rocks Paul gazed upon the vessel which had borne away Virginia, and which, now ten leagues out at sea, appeared like a black spot in the midst of the ocean. He remained a great part of the day with his eyes fixed upon this object: when it had disappeared, he still fancied he beheld it: and when, at length, the traces which clung to his imagination were lost amidst the gathering mists of the horizon, he seated himself on that wild point, forever beaten by the winds, which never cease to agitate the tops of the cabbage and gum trees, and the hoarse and moaning murmurs of which, similar to the distant sound of organs, inspire a deep melancholy. On that spot. I found Paul, with his head reclined on the rock, and his eyes fixed upon the ground. I had followed him since break of day, and after much importunity, I prevailed with him to descend from the heights, and return to his family. I conducted him to the plantation, where the first impulse of his mind, upon seeing Madame de la Tour, was to reproach her bitterly for having deceived him. Madame de la Tour told us, that a favorable wind having arose at three o'clock in the morning, and the vessel being ready to set sail, the governor, attended by his general officers, and the missionary, had come with a palanquin in search of Virginia, and that, notwithstanding her own objections, her tears, and those of Margaret, all the while exclaiming that it was for the general welfare they had carried away Virginia almost dying. 'At least,' cried Paul, 'if I had bid her farewell, I should now be more calm. I would have said to her, Virginia, if, during the time we have lived together, one word may have escaped me which has offended you, before you leave me forever, tell me that you forgive me. I would have said to her, since I am destined to see you no more, farewell, my dear Virginia, farewell! Live far from me, contented and happy!'

"When he saw that his mother and Madame de la Tour were weeping, 'You must now,' said he, 'seek some other than me to wipe away your tears;' and then, rushing out of the house, he wandered up and down the plantation. He flew eagerly to those spots which had been most dear to Virginia. He said to the goats and their kids which followed him, bleating, 'What do you ask of me? You will see her no more who used to feed you with her own hand.' He went to the bower called the Repose of Virginia; and, as the birds flew around him, exclaimed, 'Poor little birds! you will fly no more to meet her who cherished you!' and observing Fidele running backwards and forwards in search of her, he heaved a deep sigh, and cried, 'Ah! you will never find her again.' At length he went and seated himself upon the rock where he had conversed with her the preceding evening; and at the view of the ocean, upon which he had seen the vessel disappear, which bore her away, he wept bitterly.

"We continually watched his steps, apprehending some fatal consequence from the violent agitation of his mind. His mother and Madame de la Tour conjured him, in the most tender manner, not to increase their affliction by his despair. At length Madame de la Tour soothed his mind by lavishing upon him such epithets as were best calculated to revive his hopes. She called him her son, her dear son, whom she destined for her daughter. She prevailed with him to return to the house, and receive a little nourishment. He seated himself with us at table, next to the place which used to be occupied by the companion of his childhood, and, as if she had still been present, he spoke to her, and offered whatever he knew was most agreeable to her taste; and then, starting from this dream of fancy, he began to weep. For some days he employed himself in gathering together everything which had belonged to Virginia; the last nosegays she had worn, the cocoa shell in which she used to drink; and after kissing a thousand times those relics of his friend, to him the most precious treasures which the world contained, he hid them in his bosom. The spreading perfumes of the amber are not so sweet as the objects which have belonged to those we love. At length, perceiving that his anguish increased that of his mother and Madame de la Tour, and that the wants of the family required continual labor, he began, with the assistance of Domingo, to repair the garden.

"Soon after, this young man, till now indifferent as a Creole with respect to what was passing in the world, desired I would teach him to read and write, that he might carry on a correspondence with Virginia. He then wished to be instructed in geography, in order that he might form a just idea of the country where she had disembarked; and in history, that he might know the manners of the society in which she was placed. The powerful sentiment of love, which directed his present studies, had already taught him the arts of agriculture, and the manner of laying out the most irregular grounds with advantage and beauty. It must be admitted, that to the fond dreams of this restless and ardent passion, mankind are indebted for a great number of arts and sciences, while its disappointments have given birth to philosophy, which teaches us to bear the evils of life with resignation. Thus, nature having made love the general link which binds all beings, has rendered it the first spring of society, the first incitement of knowledge as well as pleasure.

"Paul found little satisfaction in the study of geography, which, instead of describing the natural history of each country, only gave a view of its political boundaries. History, and especially modern history, interested him little more. He there saw only general and periodical evils of which he did not discern the cause; wars for which there was no reason and no object; nations without principle, and princes without humanity. He preferred the reading of romances, which being filled with the particular feelings and interests of men, represented situations similar to his own. No book gave him so much pleasure as Telemachus, from the pictures which it draws of pastoral life, and of those passions which are natural to the human heart. He read aloud to his mother and Madame de la Tour those parts which affected him most sensibly, when, sometimes, touched by the most tender remembrances, his emotion choked his utterance, and his eyes were bathed in tears. He fancied he had found in Virginia the wisdom of Antiope, with the misfortunes and the tenderness of Eurcharis. With very different sensations he perused our fashionable novels, filled with licentious maxims and manners. And when he was informed that those romances drew a just picture of European society, he trembled, not without reason, lest Virginia should become corrupted, and should forget him.

"More than a year and a half had indeed passed away before Madame de la Tour received any tidings of her daughter. During that period she had only accidentally heard that Virginia had arrived safely in France. At length a vessel, which stopped in its way to the Indies, conveyed to Madame de la Tour a packet, and a letter written with her own hand. Although this amiable young woman had written in a guarded manner, in order to avoid wounding the feelings of a mother, it was easy to discern that she was unhappy. Her letter paints so naturally her situation and her character, that I have retained it almost word for word.

"'My dear and beloved mother, I have already sent you several letters, written with my own hand but having received no answer, I fear they have not reached you. I have better hopes for this, from the means I have now taken of sending you tidings of myself, and of hearing from you. I have shed many tears since our separation; I, who never used to weep, but for the misfortunes of others! My aunt was much astonished, when, having, upon my arrival, inquired what accomplishments I possessed, I told her that I could neither read nor write. She asked me what then I had learnt since I came into the world; and, when I answered that I had been taught to take care of the household affairs, and obey your will, she told me that I had received the education of a servant. The next day she placed me as a boarder in a great abbey near Paris, where I have masters of all kinds, who teach me, among other things, history, geography, grammar, mathematics and riding. But I have so little capacity for all those sciences, that I make but small progress with my masters.

"'My aunt's kindness, however, does not abate towards me. She gives me new dresses for each season; and she has placed two waiting women with me, who are both dressed like fine ladies. She has made me take the title of countess, but has obliged me to renounce the name of La Tour, which is as dear to me as it is to you, from all you have told me of the sufferings my father endured in order to marry you. She has replaced your name by that of your family, which is also dear

to me, because it was your name when a girl. Seeing
myself in so splendid a situation, I implored her to let
me send you some assistance. But how shall I repeat
her answer? Yet you have desired me always to tell you
the truth. She told me then, that a little would be of
no use to you, and that a great deal would only encum-
ber you in the simple life you led.

"'I endeavored, upon my arrival, to send you tidings
of myself by another hand, but finding no person here
in whom I could place confidence, I applied night and
day to reading and writing; and Heaven, who saw my
motive for learning, no doubt assisted my endeavors,
for I acquired both in a short time. I entrusted my first
letters to some of the ladies here, who, I have reason
to think, carried them to my aunt. This time I have
had recourse to a boarder, who is my friend. I send you
her direction, by means of which I shall receive your
answer. My aunt has forbid my holding any correspondence whatever, which might, she says, be come an
obstacle to the great views she has for my advantage.
No person is allowed to see me at the grate but herself,
and an old nobleman, one of her friends, who, she
says, is much pleased with me. I am sure I am not at
all so with him; nor should I, even if it were possible
for me to be pleased with anyone at present.

"'I live in the midst of affluence, and have not a livre
at my disposal. They say I might make an improper
use of money. Even my clothes belong to my waiting
women who quarrel about them before I have left them
off. In the bosom of riches, I am poorer than when I
lived with you; for I have nothing to give. When I
found that the great accomplishments they taught me
would not procure me the power of doing the smallest
good, I had recourse to my needle, of which happily
you had learnt me the use. I send several pair of
stockings of my own making for you and my mamma

Margaret, a cap for Domingo, and one of my red handkerchiefs for Mary. I also send with this packet some kernels and seeds of various kinds of fruits, which I gathered in the fields. There are much more beautiful flowers in the meadows of this country than in ours, but nobody cares for them. I am sure that you and my mamma Margaret will be better pleased with this bag of seeds, than you were with the bag of piastres, which was the cause of our separation and of my tears. It will give me great delight if you should one day see apple trees growing at the side of the plantain, and elms blending their foliage with our cocoa trees. You will fancy yourself in Normandy, which you love so much.

"'You desired me to relate to you my joys and my griefs. I have no joys far from you. As for my griefs, I endeavor to soothe them by reflecting that I am in the situation in which you placed me by the will of God. But my greatest affliction is, that no one here speaks to me of you, and that I must speak of you to no one. My waiting women, or rather those of my aunt, for they belong more to her than to me, told me the other day, when I wished to turn the conversation upon the objects most dear to me, 'Remember, madam, that you are a Frenchwoman, and must forget that country of savages.' Ah! sooner will I forget myself than forget the spot on which I was born, and which you inhabit! It is this country which is to me a land of savages; for I live alone, having no one to whom I can impart, those feelings of tenderness for you which I shall bear with me to the grave.

'I am,
'My dearest and beloved mother,
'Your affectionate and dutiful daughter,
'VIRGINIA DE LA TOUR"

"'I recommend to your goodness Mary and Dom-

ingo, who took so much care of my infancy. Caress
Fidele for me who found me in the wood.'

"Paul was astonished that Virginia had not said one
word of him, she who had not forgotten even the house
dog. But Paul was not aware that, however long may
be a woman's letter, she always puts the sentiments
most dear to her at the end.

"In a postscript, Virginia recommended particularly
to Paul's care two kinds of seed, those of the violet and
scabious. She gave him some instructions upon the
nature of those plants, and the spots most proper for
their cultivation. 'The first,' said she, 'produces a little
flower of a deep violet, which loves to hide itself
beneath the bushes, but is soon discovered by its delightful odors.' She desired those seeds might be sown
along the borders of the fountain, at the foot of her
cocoa tree. 'The scabious,' she added, 'produces a beautiful flower of a pale blue, and a black ground, spotted
with white. You might fancy it was in mourning; and
for this reason, it is called the widow's flower. It de-
lights in bleak spots beaten by the winds.' She begged
this might be sown upon the rock where she had
spoken to him for the last time, and that, for her sake,
he would henceforth give it the name of the Farewell
Rock.

"She had put those seeds into a little purse, the tissue
of which was extremely simple; but which appeared
above all price to Paul, when he perceived a P and a V
entwined together, and knew that the beautiful hair
which formed the cipher was the hair of Virginia.

"The whole family listened with tears to the letter of
that amiable and virtuous young woman. Her mother
answered it in the name of the little society, and desired
her to remain or return as she thought proper; assuring
her, that happiness had fled from their dwelling since
her departure, and that, as for herself, she was incon-

solable.

"Paul also sent her a long letter, in which he assured her that he would arrange the garden in a manner agreeable to her taste, and blend the plants of Europe with those of Africa. He sent her some fruit culled from the cocoa trees of the mountain, which were now arrived at maturity: telling her that he would not add anymore of the other seeds of the island, that the desire of seeing those productions again might hasten her return. He conjured her to comply without delay with the ardent wishes of her family, and, above all, with his own, since he was unable to endure the pain of their separation.

"With a careful hand Paul sowed the European seeds, particularly the violet and the scabious, the flowers of which seem to bear some analogy to the character and situation of Virginia, by whom they had been recommended: but whether they were injured by the voyage, or whether the soil of this part of Africa is unfavorable to their growth, a very small number of them blew, and none came to perfection.

"Meanwhile that envy, which pursues human happiness, spread reports over the island which gave great uneasiness to Paul. The persons who had brought Virginia's letter asserted that she was upon the point of being married, and named the nobleman of the court with whom she was going to be united. Some even declared that she was already married, of which they were witnesses. Paul at first despised this report, brought by one of those trading ships, which often spread erroneous intelligence in their passage; but some ill-natured persons, by their insulting pity, led him to give some degree of credit to this cruel intelligence. Besides, he had seen in the novels which he had lately read that perfidy was treated as a subject of pleasantry; and knowing that those books were faithful representations of European manners, he feared that the heart of Virginia was corrupted, and had forgotten its former engagements. Thus his acquirements only served to render him miserable, and what increased his apprehension was, that several ships arrived from Europe, during the space of six months, and not one brought any tidings of Virginia.

"This unfortunate young man, with a heart torn by the most cruel agitation, came often to visit me, that I might confirm or banish his inquietude, by my experience of the world.

"I live, as I have already told you, a league and a half from hence, upon the banks of a little river which glides along the Sloping Mountain: there I lead a solitary life, without wife, children, or slaves.

"After having enjoyed, and lost, the rare felicity of living with a congenial mind, the state of life which appears the least wretched is that of solitude. It is remarkable that all those nations which have been rendered unhappy by their political opinions, their manners, or their forms of government, have produced numerous classes of citizens altogether devoted to solitude and celibacy. Such were the Egyptians in their decline, the Greeks of the lower empire; and such in our days are the Indians, the Chinese, the modern Greeks, the Italians, and most part of the eastern and southern nations of Europe.

"Thus I pass my days far from mankind whom I wished to serve, and by whom I have been persecuted. After having traveled over many countries of Europe, and some parts of America and Africa, I at length pitched my tent in this thinly-peopled island, allured by its mild temperature and its solitude. A cottage which I built in the woods, at the foot of a tree, a little field which I cultivated with my own hands, a river which glides before my door, suffice for my wants and

for my pleasures. I blend with those enjoyments that
of some chosen books, which teach me to become
better. They make that world, which I have abandoned,
still contribute to my satisfaction. They place before
me pictures of those passions which render its inhabitants so miserable; and the comparison which I make
between their destiny and my own, leads me to feel a
sort of negative happiness. Like a man whom ship-
wreck has thrown upon a rock, I contemplate, from
my solitude, the storms which roll over the rest of the
world; and my repose seems more profound from the
distant sounds of the tempest.

"I suffer myself to be led calmly down the stream of
time to the ocean of futurity, which has no boundaries;
while, in the contemplation of the present harmony
of nature, I raise my soul towards its supreme Author,
and hope for a more happy destiny in another state of
existence.

"Although you do not descry my hermitage, which
is situated in the midst of a forest, among that immense
variety of objects which this elevated spot presents, the
grounds are disposed with particular beauty, at least to
one who, like me, loves rather the seclusion of a home
scene, than great and extensive prospects. The river
which glides before my door passes in a straight line
across the woods, and appears like a long canal shaded
by trees of all kinds. There are black date plum trees,
what we here call the narrow-leaved dodonea, olive
wood, gum trees, and the cinnamon tree; while in some
parts the cabbage trees raise their naked columns more
than a hundred feet high, crowned at their summits
with clustering leaves, and towering above the wood
like one forest piled upon another. Lianas, of various
foliage, intertwining among the woods, form arcades
of flowers, and verdant canopies; those trees, for the
most part, shed aromatic odors of a nature so powerful,

that the garments of a traveler, who has passed through the forest, retain for several hours the delicious fragrance. In the season when those trees produce their lavish blossoms, they appear as if covered with snow. One of the principal ornaments of our woods is the calbassia, a tree not only distinguished for its beautiful tint of verdure; but for other properties, which Madame de la Tour has described in the following sonnet, written at one of her first visits to my hermitage:

SONNET
TO THE CALBASSIA TREE

Sublime Calbassia, luxuriant tree!
How soft the gloom thy bright-lined foliage throws,
While from thy pulp a healing balsam flows,
Whose power the suffering wretch from pain can
      free!
My pensive footsteps ever turn to thee!
Since oft, while musing on my lasting woes,
Beneath thy flowery white bells I repose,
Symbol of friendship dost thou seem to me;
For thus has friendship cast her soothing shade
O'er my unsheltered bosom's keen distress:
Thus sought to heal the wounds which love has
      made,
And temper bleeding sorrow's sharp excess!
Ah! not in vain she lends her balmy aid:
The agonies she cannot cure, are less!

"Towards the end of summer various kinds of foreign birds hasten, impelled by an inexplicable instinct, from unknown regions, and across immense oceans, to gather the profuse grains of this island; and the brilliancy of their expanded plumage forms a contrast to the trees embrowned by the sun. Such, among others, are various kinds of parakeets, the blue pigeon, called here the pigeon of Holland, and the wandering and majestic white bird of the Tropic, which Madame de la Tour thus apostrophized: —

SONNET
TO THE WHITE BIRD OF THE TROPIC

Bird of the Tropic! thou, who lov'st to stray
Where thy long pinions sweep the sultry line,
Or mark'st the bounds which torrid beams confine
By thy averted course, that shuns the ray
Oblique, enamor'd of sublimer day:
Oft on yon cliff thy folded plumes recline,
And drop those snowy feathers Indians twine
To crown the warrior's brow with honors gay.
O'er Trackless oceans what impels thy wing?
Does no soft instinct in thy soul prevail?
No sweet affection to thy bosom cling,
And bid thee oft thy absent nest bewail?
Yet thou again to that dear spot canst spring
But I my long lost home no more shall hail!

"The domestic inhabitants of our forests, monkeys, sport upon the dark branches of the trees, from which they are distinguished by their gray and greenish skin, and their black visages. Some hang suspended by the tail, and balance themselves in air; others leap from branch to branch, bearing their young in their arms. The murderous gun has never affrighted those peaceful children of nature. You sometimes hear the warblings of unknown birds from the southern countries, repeated at a distance by the echoes of the forest. The river, which runs in foaming cataracts over a bed of rocks, reflects here and there, upon its limpid waters, venerable masses of woody shade, together with the sport of its happy inhabitants. About a thousand paces from thence the river precipitates itself over several piles of rocks, and forms, in its fall, a sheet of water smooth as crystal, but which breaks at the bottom into frothy surges. Innumerable confused sounds issue from those tumultuous waters, which, scattered by the winds of the forest, sometimes sink, sometimes swell, and send forth a hollow tone like the deep bells of a cathedral. The air, forever renewed by the circulation of the waters, fans the banks of that river with freshness, and leaves a degree of verdure, notwithstanding the summer heats, rarely found in this island, even upon the summits of the mountains.

"At some distance is a rock, placed far enough from the cascade to prevent the ear from being deafened by the noise of its waters, and sufficiently near for the enjoyment of their view, their coolness, and their murmurs. Thither, amidst the heats of summer, Madame de la Tour, Margaret, Virginia, Paul, and myself sometimes repaired, and dined beneath the shadow of the rock. Virginia, who always directed her most ordinary actions to the good of others, never ate of any fruit without planting the seed or kernel in the ground. 'From this,' said she, 'trees will come, which will give their fruit to some traveler, or at least to some bird.'

One day having eaten of the papaw fruit, at the foot
of that rock she planted the seeds. Soon after several
papaws sprung up, amongst which was one that yielded
fruit. This tree had risen but a little from the ground
at the time of Virginia's departure; but its growth being
rapid, in the space of two years it had gained twenty
feet of height, and the upper part of its stem was
encircled with several layers of ripe fruit. Paul having
wandered to that spot, was delighted to see that this
lofty tree had arisen from the small seed planted by his
beloved friend; but that emotion instantly gave place
to a deep melancholy, at this evidence of her long
absence. The objects which we see habitually do not
remind us of the rapidity of life; they decline insensibly
with ourselves; but those which we behold again, after
having for some years lost sight of them, impress us
powerfully with the idea of that swiftness with which
the tide of our days flows on. Paul was no less overwhelmed and affected at the sight of this great papaw
tree, loaded with fruit, than is the traveler, when, after
a long absence from his own country, he finds not his
contemporaries, but their children, whom he left at the
breast, and whom he sees are become fathers of families. Paul sometimes thought of hewing down the tree,
which recalled too sensibly the distracted image of that
length of time which had clasped since the departure
of Virginia. Sometimes, contemplating it as a monument of her benevolence, he kissed its trunk, and
apostrophized it in terms of the most passionate regret;
and, indeed I have myself gazed upon it with more
emotion and more veneration than upon the trium-
phal arches of Rome.

"At the foot of this papaw I was always sure to meet
with Paul when he came into our neighborhood. One
day, when I found him absorbed in melancholy, we
had a conversation, which I will relate to you, if I do

not weary you by my long digressions; perhaps pardonable to my age and my last friendships.

"Paul said to me, 'I am very unhappy. Mademoiselle de la Tour has now been gone two years and two months; and we have heard no tidings of her for eight months and two weeks. She is rich, and I am poor. She has forgotten me. I have a great mind to follow her. I will go to France; I will serve the king; make a fortune; and then Mademoiselle de la Tour's aunt will bestow her niece upon me when I shall have become a great lord.

"'But, my dear friend,' I answered, 'have you not told me that you are not of noble birth?'

"'My mother has told me so,' said Paul. 'As for myself I know not what noble birth means.'

"'Obscure birth,' I replied, 'in France shuts out all access to great employments; nor can you even be received among any distinguished body of men.'

"'How unfortunate I am!' resumed Paul; 'everything repulses me. I am condemned to waste my wretched life in labor, far from Virginia.' And he heaved a deep sigh.

"'Since her relation,' he added, 'will only give her in marriage to some one with a great name, by the aid of study we become wise and celebrated. I will fly then to study; I will acquire sciences; I will serve my country usefully by my attainments; I shall be independent; I shall become renowned; and my glory will belong only to myself.'

"'My son! talents are still more rare than birth or riches, and are undoubtedly an inestimable good, of which nothing can deprive us, and which everywhere conciliate public esteem. But they cost dear: they are generally allied to exquisite sensibility, which renders their possessor miserable. But you tell me that you would serve mankind. He who, from the soil which he cultivates, draws forth one additional sheaf of corn, serves mankind more than he who presents them with a book.'

"'Oh! she then,' exclaimed Paul, 'who planted this papaw tree, made a present to the inhabitants of the forest more dear and more useful than if she had given them a library.' And seizing the tree in his arms, he kissed it with transport.

"'Ah! I desire glory only,' he resumed, 'to confer it upon Virginia, and render her dear to the whole universe. But you, who know so much, tell me if we shall ever be married. I wish I was at least learned enough to look into futurity. Virginia must come back. What need has she of a rich relation? she was so happy in those huts, so beautiful, and so well dressed, with a red handkerchief or flowers round her head! Return, Virginia! Leave your palaces, your splendor! Return to these rocks, to the shade of our woods and our cocoa trees! Alas! you are, perhaps, unhappy!' And he began to weep. 'My father! conceal nothing from me. If you cannot tell me whether I shall marry Virginia or no, tell me, at least, if she still loves me amidst those great lords who speak to the king, and go to see her.'

"'Oh! my dear friend,' I answered, 'I am sure that she loves you, for several reasons; but, above all, because she is virtuous.' At those words he threw himself upon my neck in a transport of joy.

"'But what,' said he, 'do you understand by virtue?'

"'My son! to you, who support your family by your labor, it need not be defined. Virtue is an effort which we make for the good of others, and with the intention of pleasing God.'

"'Oh! how virtuous then,' cried he, 'is Virginia! Virtue made her seek for riches, that she might practice benevolence. Virtue led her to forsake this island, and virtue will bring her back.' The idea of her near return fired his imagination, and his inquietudes suddenly vanished. Virginia, he was persuaded, had not written, because she would soon arrive. It took so little time to come from Europe with a fair wind! Then he enumerated the vessels which had made a passage of four thousand five hundred leagues in less than three months; and perhaps the vessel in which Virginia had embarked might not be longer than two. Ship builders were now so ingenious, and sailors so expert! He then told me of the arrangements he would make for her reception, of the new habitation he would build for her, of the pleasures and surprises which each day should bring along with it when she was his wife? His wife! That hope was ecstasy. 'At least, my dear father,' said he, 'you shall then do nothing more than you please. Virginia being rich, we shall have a number of Negroes, who will labor for you. You shall always live with us, and have no other care than to amuse and rejoice yourself.' and, his heart throbbing with delight, he flew to communicate those exquisite sensations to his family.

"In a short time, however, the most cruel apprehensions succeeded those enchanting hopes. Violent passions ever throw the soul into opposite extremes. Paul returned to my dwelling absorbed in melancholy, and said to me, 'I hear nothing from Virginia. Had she left Europe she would have informed me of her departure. Ah! the reports which I have heard concerning her are but too well founded. Her aunt has married her to some great lord. She, like others, has been undone by the love of riches. In those books which paint women so well, virtue is but a subject of romance. Had Virginia been virtuous, she would not have forsaken her mother and me, and, while I pass life in thinking of her, forgotten me. While I am wretched, she is happy. Ah! that thought distracts me: labor becomes painful, and society irksome. Would to heaven that war were declared in India! I would go there and die.'

"'My son,' I answered, 'that courage which, prompts us to court death is but the courage of a moment, and is often excited by the vain hopes of posthumous fame. There is a species of courage more necessary, and more rare, which makes us support, without witness, and without applause, the various vexations of life; and that is, patience. Leaning not upon the opinions of others, but upon the will of God, patience is the courage of virtue.'

"'Ah!' cried he,' I am then without virtue! Everything overwhelms and distracts me.'

"'Equal, constant, and invariable virtue,' I replied, 'belongs not to man.' In the midst of so many passions, by which we are agitated, our reason is disordered and obscured: but there is an ever-burning lamp, at which we can rekindle its flame; and that is, literature.

"'Literature, my dear son, is the gift of Heaven; a ray of that wisdom which governs the universe; and which man, inspired by celestial intelligence, has drawn down to earth. Like the sun, it enlightens, it rejoices, it warms with a divine flame, and seems, in some sort, like the element of fire, to bend all nature to our use. By the aid of literature, we bring around us all things, all places, men, and times. By its aid we calm the passions, suppress vice, and excite virtue. Literature is the daughter of heaven, who has descended upon earth to soften and to charm all human evils.

"'Have recourse to your books, then, my son. The sages who have written before our days, are travelers who have preceded us in the paths of misfortune; who stretch out a friendly hand towards us, and invite us to join their society, when everything else abandons us. A good book is a good friend.'

"'Ah!' cried Paul, 'I stood in no need of books when

Virginia was here, and she had studied as little as me: but when she looked at me, and called me her friend, it was impossible for me to be unhappy.'

"'Undoubtedly,' said I, 'there is no friend so agreeable as a mistress by whom we are beloved. There is in the gay graces of a woman a charm that dispels the dark phantoms of reflection. Upon her face sits soft attraction and tender confidence. What joy is not heightened in which she shares? What brow is not unbent by her smiles? What anger can resist her tears? Virginia will return with more philosophy than you, and will be surprised not to find the garden finished: she who thought of its establishments amidst the persecutions of her aunt, and far from her mother and from you.'

"The idea of Virginia's speedy return reanimated her lover's courage, and he resumed his pastoral occupations; happy amidst his toils, in the reflection that they would find a termination so dear to the wishes of his heart.

"The 24th of December, 1774, at break of day, Paul, when he arose, perceived a white flag hoisted upon the Mountain of Discovery, which was the signal of a vessel descried at sea. He flew to the town, in order to learn if this vessel brought any tidings of Virginia, and waited till the return of the pilot, who had gone as usual to visit the ship. The pilot brought the governor information that the vessel was the Saint Geran, of seven hundred tons, commanded by a captain of the name of Aubin; that the ship was now four leagues out at sea, and would anchor at Port Louis the following afternoon, if the wind was favorable: at present there was a calm. The pilot then remitted to the governor a number of letters from France, amongst which was one addressed to Madame de la Tour in the hand-writing of Virginia. Paul seized upon the letter, kissed it with transport, placed it in his bosom, and flew to the plantation. No sooner did he perceive from a distance the family, who were waiting his return upon the Farewell Rock, than he waved the letter in the air, without having the power to speak; and instantly the whole family crowded round Madame de la Tour to hear it read. Virginia informed her mother that she had suffered much ill treatment from her aunt, who, after having in vain urged her to marry against her inclination, had disinherited her; and at length sent her back at such a season of the year, that she must probably reach the Mauritius at the very period of the hurricanes. In vain, she added, she had endeavored to soften her aunt, by representing what she owed to her mother, and to the habits of her early years: she had been treated as a romantic girl, whose head was turned by novels. At present she said she could think of nothing but the transport of again seeing and embracing her beloved family, and that she would have satisfied this dearest wish of her heart that very day, if the captain would have permitted her to embark in the pilot's boat; but that he had opposed her going, on account of the distance from the shore, and of a swell in the ocean, notwithstanding it was a calm.

"Scarcely was the letter finished, when the whole family, transported with joy repeated, 'Virginia is arrived!' and mistresses and servants embraced each other. Madame de la Tour said to Paul, 'My son, go and inform our neighbor of Virginia's arrival.' Domingo immediately lighted a torch, and he and Paul bent their way towards my plantation.

"It was about ten at night, and I was going to extinguish my lamp, when I perceived through the palisades of my hut a light in the woods. I arose, and had just dressed myself when Paul, half wild, and panting for breath, sprung on my neck, crying, 'Come along, come along. Virginia is arrived! Let us go to the Port: the vessel will anchor at break of day.'

"We instantly set off. As we were traversing the woods of the Sloping Mountain, and were already on the road which leads from the Shaddock Grove to the Port, I heard some one walking behind us. When the person, who was a Negro, and who advanced with hasty steps, had reached us, I inquired from whence he came, and whither he was going with such expedition. He answered, 'I come from that part of the island called Golden Dust, and am sent to the Port, to inform the governor, that a ship from France has anchored upon the island of Amber, and fires guns of distress, for the sea is very stormy.' Having said this, the man left us, and pursued his journey.

"'Let us go,' said I to Paul, 'towards that part of the island, and meet Virginia. It is only three leagues from hence.' Accordingly we bent our course thither. The heat was suffocating. The moon had risen, and it was encompassed by three large black circles. A dismal darkness shrouded the sky; but the frequent flakes of lightning discovered long chains of thick clouds, gloomy, low hung, and heaped together over the middle of the island, after having rolled with great rapidity from the ocean, although we felt not a breath of wind upon the land. As we walked along we thought we heard peals of thunder; but, after listening more attentively, we found they were the sound of distant cannon repeated by the echoes. Those sounds, joined to the tempestuous aspect of the heavens, made me shudder. I had little doubt that they were signals of distress from a ship in danger. In half an hour the firing ceased, and I felt the silence more appalling than the dismal sounds which had preceded.

"We hastened on without uttering a word, or daring to communicate our apprehensions. At midnight we arrived on the seashore at that part of the island. The billows broke against the beach with a horrible noise, covering the rocks and the strand with their foam of a dazzling whiteness, and blended with sparks of fire. By their phosphoric gleams we distinguished, notwithstanding the darkness, the canoes of the fishermen, which they had drawn far upon the sand.

"Near the shore, at the entrance of a wood, we saw a fire, round which several of the inhabitants were assembled. Thither we repaired, in order to repose ourselves till morning. One of the circle related, that in the afternoon he had seen a vessel driven towards the island by the currents; that the night had hid it from his view; and that two hours after sun-set he had heard the firing of guns in distress; but that the sea was so tempestuous, no boat could venture out; that a short time after, he thought he perceived the glimmering of the watch-lights on board the vessel, which he feared, by its having approached so near the coast, had steered between the main land and the little island of Amber, mistaking it for the point of Endeavor, near which the vessels pass in order to gain Port Louis. If this was the case, which, however, he could not affirm, the ship he apprehended was in great danger. Another islander then informed us, that he had frequently crossed the channel which separates the isle of Amber from the coast, and which he had sounded; that the anchorage was good, and that the ship would there be in as great security as if it were in harbor. A third islander declared it was impossible for the ship to enter that channel, which was scarcely navigable for a boat. He asserted that he had seen the vessel at anchor beyond the isle of Amber; so that if the wind arose in the morning, it could either put to sea or gain the harbor. Different opinions were stated upon this subject, which, while those indolent Creoles calmly discussed, Paul and I observed a profound silence. We remained on this spot till break of day, when the weather was too hazy to admit of our distinguishing any object at sea, which was covered with fog. All we could descry was a dark cloud, which they told us was the isle of Amber, at the distance of a quarter of a league from the coast. We could only discern on this gloomy day the point of the beach where we stood, and the peaks of some mountains in the interior part of the island, rising occasionally from amidst the clouds which hung around them.

"At seven in the morning we heard the beat of drums in the woods; and soon after the governor, Monsieur de la Bourdonnais, arrived on horseback, followed by a detachment of soldiers armed with muskets, and a great number of islanders and blacks. He ranged his soldiers upon the beach, and ordered them to make a general discharge, which was no sooner done, than we perceived a glimmering light upon the water, which was instantly succeeded by the sound of a gun. We judged that the ship was at no great distance, and ran towards that part where we had seen the light. We now discerned through the fog the hull and tackling of a large vessel; and notwithstanding the noise of the waves, we were near enough to hear the whistle of the boatswain at the helm, and the shouts of the mariners. As soon as the Saint Geran perceived that we were enough to give her succor, she continued to fire guns regularly at the interval of three minutes. Monsieur de la Bourdonnais caused great fires to be lighted at certain distances upon the strand, and sent to all the inhabitants of that neighborhood, in search of provisions, planks, cables, and empty barrels. A crowd of people soon arrived, accompanied by their Negroes, loaded with provisions and rigging. One of the most aged of the planters approaching the governor, said to him, 'We have heard all night hoarse noises in the

mountain, and in the forests: the leaves of the trees are
shaken, although there is no wind: the sea birds seek
refuge upon the land: it is certain that all those signs
announce a hurricane.' 'Well, my friends,' answered the
governor, 'we are prepared for it: and no doubt the
vessel is also.'

"Everything, indeed, presaged the near approach of
the hurricane. The center of the clouds in the zenith
was of a dismal black, while their skirts were fringed
with a copper hue. The air resounded with the cries of
the frigate bird, the cur water, and a multitude of other
sea birds, who, notwithstanding the obscurity of the
atmosphere, hastened from all points of the horizon
to seek for shelter in the island.

"Towards nine in the morning we heard on the side
of the ocean the most terrific noise, as if torrents of
water, mingled with thunder, were rolling down the
steeps of the mountains. A general cry was heard of,
'There is the hurricane!' and in one moment a frightful
whirlwind scattered the fog which had covered the Isle
of Amber and its channel. The Saint Geran then presented itself to our view, her gallery crowded with
people, her yards and main topmast laid upon the
deck, her flag shivered, with four cables at her head,
and one by which she was held at the stern. She had
anchored between the Isle of Amber and the main land,
within that chain of breakers which encircles the island, and which bar she had passed over, in a place
where no vessel had ever gone before. She presented
her head to the waves which rolled from the open sea;
and as each billow rushed into the straits, the ship
heaved, so that her keel was in air; and at the same
moment her stern, plunging into the water, disappeared altogether, as if it were swallowed up by the
surges. In this position, driven by the winds and waves
towards the shore, it was equally impossible for her to

return by the passage through which she had made her way; or, by cutting her cables, to throw herself upon the beach, from which she was separated by sandbanks, mingled with breakers. Every billow which broke upon the coast advanced roaring to the bottom of the bay, and threw planks to the distance of fifty feet upon the land; then rushing back, laid bare its sandy bed, from which it rolled immense stones, with a hoarse dismal noise. The sea, swelled by the violence of the wind, rose higher every moment; and the channel between this island the Isle of Amber was but one vast sheet of white foam, with yawning pits of black deep billows. The foam boiling in the gulf was more than six feet high: and the winds which swept its surface, bore it over the steep coast more than half a league upon the land. Those innumerable white flakes, driven horizontally as far as the foot of the mountain, appeared like snow issuing from the ocean, which was now confounded with the sky. Thick clouds, of a horrible form, swept along the zenith with the swiftness of birds, while others appeared motionless as rocks. No spot of azure could be discerned in the firmament; only a pale yellow gleam displayed the objects of earth sea, and skies.

"From the violent efforts of the ship, what we dreaded happened. The cables at the head of the vessel were torn away; it was then held by one anchor only, and was instantly dashed upon the rocks, at the distance of half a cable's length from the shore. A general cry of horror issued from the spectators. Paul rushed towards the sea, when, seizing him by the arm, I exclaimed, 'Would you perish?' — 'Let me go to save her,' cried he, 'or die!' Seeing that despair deprived him of reason, Domingo and I, in order to preserve him, fastened a long cord round his waist, and seized hold of each end. Paul then precipitated himself towards the ship, now swimming, and now walking upon the break-

ers. Sometimes he had the hope of reaching the vessel,
which the sea, in its irregular movements, had left
almost dry, so that you could have made its circuit on
foot; but suddenly the waves advancing with new fury,
shrouded it beneath mountains of water, which then
lifted it upright upon its keel. The billows at the same
moment threw the unfortunate Paul far upon the
beach, his legs bathed in blood, his bosom wounded,
and himself half dead. The moment he had recovered
his senses, he arose, and returned with new ardor towards the vessel, the planks of which now yawned
asunder from the violent strokes of the billows. The
crew, then despairing of their safety, threw themselves
in crowds into the sea, upon yards, planks, hencoops,
tables, and barrels. At this moment we beheld an object
fitted to excite eternal sympathy; a young lady in the
gallery of the stern of the Saint Geran, stretching out
her arms towards him who made so many efforts to
join her. It was Virginia. She had discovered her lover
by his intrepidity. The sight of this amiable young
woman, exposed to such horrible danger, filled us with
unutterable despair. As for Virginia, with a firm and
dignified mien, she waved her hand, as if bidding us
an eternal farewell. All the sailors had flung themselves
into the sea, except one, who still remained upon the
deck, and who was naked, and strong as Hercules. This
man approached Virginia with respect, and, kneeling
at her feet attempted to force her to throw off her
clothes; but she repulsed him with modesty, and
turned away her head. Then was heard redoubled cries
from the spectators, 'Save her! Save her! Do not leave
her!' But at that moment a mountain billow, of enor-
mous magnitude, engulfed itself between the Isle of
Amber and the coast, and menaced the shattered vessel,
towards which it rolled bellowing, with its black sides
and foaming head. At this terrible sight the sailor flung

himself into the sea; and Virginia seeing death inevitable, placed one hand upon her clothes, the other on her heart, and lifting up her lovely eyes, seemed an angel prepared to take her flight to heaven.

"Oh, day of horror! Alas! everything was swallowed up by the relentless billows. The surge threw some of the spectators far upon the beach, whom an impulse of humanity prompted to advance towards Virginia, and also the sailor who had endeavored to save her life. This man, who had escaped from almost certain death, kneeling on the sand, exclaimed, 'Oh, my God! thou hast saved my life, but I would have given it willingly for that poor young woman!'

"Domingo and myself drew Paul senseless to the shore, the blood flowing from his mouth and ears. The governor put him into the hands of a surgeon, while we sought along the beach for the corpse of Virginia. But the wind having suddenly changed, which frequently happens during hurricanes, our search was in vain; and we lamented that we could not even pay this unfortunate young woman the last sad sepulchral duties.

"We retired from the spot overwhelmed with dismay, and our minds wholly occupied by one cruel loss, although numbers had perished in the wreck. Some of the spectators seemed tempted, from the fatal destiny of this virtuous young woman, to doubt the existence of Providence. Alas! there are in life such terrible, such unmerited evils, that even the hope of the wise is sometimes shaken.

"In the meantime, Paul, who began to recover his senses, was taken to a house in the neighborhood, till he was able to be removed to his own habitation. Thither I bent my way with Domingo, and undertook the sad task of preparing Virginia's mother and her friend for the melancholy event which had happened.

When we reached the entrance of the valley of the river of Fan-Palms, some Negroes informed us that the sea had thrown many pieces of the wreck into the opposite bay. We descended towards it; and one of the first objects which struck my sight upon the beach was the corpse of Virginia. The body was half covered with sand, and in the attitude in which we had seen her perish. Her features were not changed; her eyes were closed, her countenance was still serene; but the pale violets of death were blended on her cheek with the blush of virgin modesty. One of her hands was placed upon her clothes: and the other, which she held on her heart, was fast closed, and so stiffened, that it was with difficulty I took from its grasp a small box. How great was my emotion, when I saw it contained the picture of Paul; which she had promised him never to part with while she lived! At the sight of this last mark of the fidelity and tenderness of the unfortunate girl, I wept bitterly. As for Domingo, he beat his breast, and pierced the air with his cries. We carried the body of Virginia to a fisher's hut, and gave it in charge to some poor Malabar women, who carefully washed away the sand.

"While they were employed in this melancholy office, we ascended with trembling steps to the plantation. We found Madame de la Tour and Margaret at prayer, while waiting for tidings from the ship. As soon as Madame de la Tour saw me coming, she eagerly cried, 'Where is my child, my dear child?' My silence and my tears apprised her of her misfortune. She was seized with convulsive stiflings, with agonizing pains, and her voice was only heard in groans. Margaret cried, 'Where is my son? I do not see my son!' and fainted. We ran to her assistance. In a short time she recovered, and being assured that her son was safe, and under the care of the governor, she only thought of succoring her friend, who had long successive faintings. Madame de la Tour passed the night in sufferings so exquisite, that I became convinced there was no sorrow like a mother's sorrow. When she recovered her senses, she cast her languid and steadfast looks on heaven. In vain her friend and myself pressed her hands in ours: in vain we called upon her by the most tender names; she appeared wholly insensible; and her oppressed bosom heaved deep and hollow moans.

"In the morning Paul was brought home in a palanquin. He was now restored to reason but unable to utter a word. His interview with his mother and Madame de la Tour, which I had dreaded, produced a better effect than all my cares. A ray of consolation gleamed upon the countenances of those unfortunate mothers. They flew to meet him, clasped him in their arms, and bathed him with tears, which excess of anguish had till now forbidden to flow. Paul mixed his tears with theirs; and nature having thus found relief, a long stupor succeeded the convulsive pangs they had suffered, and gave them a lethargic repose like that of death.

"Monsieur de la Bourdonnais sent to apprise me secretly that the corpse of Virginia had been borne to the town by his order, from whence it was to be transferred to the church of the Shaddock Grove. I hastened to Port Louis, and found a multitude assembled from all parts, in order to be present at the funeral solemnity, as if the whole island had lost its fairest ornament. The vessels in the harbor had their yards crossed, their flags hoisted, and fired guns at intervals. The grenadiers led the funeral procession, with their muskets reversed, their drums muffled, and sending forth slow dismal sounds. Eight young ladies of the most considerable families of the island, dressed in white, and bearing palms in their hands, supported the pall of their amiable companion, which was strewed with flowers. They were followed by a band of children chanting hymns, and by the governor, his field officers, all the principal inhabitants of the island, and an immense crowd of people.

"This funeral solemnity had been ordered by the administration of the country, who were desirous of rendering honors to the virtue of Virginia. But when the progression arrived at the foot of this mountain, at the sight of those cottages, of which she had long been the ornament and happiness, and which her loss now filled with despair, the funeral pomp was interrupted, the hymns and anthems ceased, and the plain resounded with sighs and lamentations. Companies of young girls ran from the neighboring plantations to touch the coffin of Virginia with their scarves, chaplets, and crowns of flowers, invoking her as a saint. Mothers asked of heaven a child like Virginia; lovers, a heart as faithful; the poor, as tender a friend; and the slaves, as kind a mistress.

"When the procession had reached the place of interment, the Negresses of Madagascar, and the kafirs of Mozambique, placed baskets of fruit around the corpse, and hung pieces of stuff upon the neighboring trees, according to the custom of their country. The Indians of Bengal, and of the coast of Malabar, brought cages filled with birds, which they set at liberty upon her coffin. Thus did the loss of this amiable object affect the natives of different countries, and thus was the ritual of various religions breathed over the tomb of unfortunate virtue.

"She was interred near the church of the Shaddock Grove, upon the western side, at the foot of a copse of bamboos, where, in coming from mass with her mother and Margaret, she loved to repose herself, seated by him whom she called her brother.

"On his return from the funeral solemnity, Monsieur de la Bourdonnais came hither, followed by part of his numerous train. He offered Madame de la Tour and her friend all the assistance which it was in his power to bestow. After expressing his indignation at the conduct of her unnatural aunt, he advanced to Paul, and said everything which he thought most likely to soothe and console him. 'Heaven is my witness,' said he, 'that I wished to ensure your happiness, and that of your family. My dear friend, you must go to France: I will obtain a commission for you, and during your absence will take the same care of your mother as if she were my own.' He then offered him his hand; but Paul drew away, and turned his head, unable to bear his sight.

"I remained at the plantation of my unfortunate friends, that I might render to them and Paul those offices of friendship which soften, though they cannot cure, calamity. At the end of three weeks Paul was able to walk, yet his mind seemed to droop in proportion as his frame gathered strength. He was insensible to everything; his look was vacant; and when spoken to, he made no reply. Madame de la Tour, who was dying, said to him often, 'My son, while I look at you, I think I see Virginia.' At the name of Virginia he shuddered, and hastened from her, notwithstanding the entreaties of his mother, who called him back to her friend. He used to wander into the garden, and seat himself at the foot of Virginia's cocoa tree, with his eyes fixed upon the fountain. The surgeon to the governor, who had shown the most humane attention to Paul, and the whole family, told us that, in order to cure that deep melancholy which had taken possession of his mind, we must allow him to do whatever he pleased, without contradiction, as the only means of conquering his inflexible silence.

"I resolved to follow this advice. The first use which Paul made of his returning strength was to absent himself from the plantation. Being determined not to lose sight of him, I set out immediately, and desired Domingo to take some provisions and accompany us. Paul's strength and spirits seemed renewed as he descended the mountain. He took the road of the Shaddock Grove; and when he was near the church, in the Alley of Bamboos, he walked directly to the spot where he saw some new-laid earth, and there kneeling down, and raising up his eyes to heaven, he offered up a long prayer, which appeared to me a symptom of returning reason; since this mark of confidence in the Supreme Being showed that his mind began to resume its natural functions. Domingo and I followed his example, fell upon our knees, and mingled our prayers with his. When he arose, he bent his way, paying little attention to us, towards the northern part of the island. As we knew that he was not only ignorant of the spot where the body of Virginia was laid, but even whether it had been snatched from the waves, I asked him why he had offered up his prayer at the foot of those bamboos. He answered, 'We have been there so often!' He continued his course until we reached the borders of the forest, when night came on. I prevailed with him to take some nourishment; and we slept upon the grass, at the foot of a tree. The next day I thought he seemed disposed to trace back his steps; for, after having gazed a considerable time upon the church of the Shaddock Grove with its avenues of bamboo stretching along the plain, he made a motion as if he would return; but, suddenly plunging into the forest, he directed his course to the north. I judged what was his design, from which I endeavored to dissuade him in vain. At noon he arrived at that part of the island called the Gold Dust. He rushed to the seashore, opposite to the spot where the Saint Geran perished. At the sight of the Isle of Amber and its channel, then smooth as a mirror, he cried, 'Virginia! Oh, my dear Virginia!' and fell senseless. Domingo and myself carried him into the woods, where we recovered him with some difficulty. He made an effort to return to the seashore; but, having conjured him not to renew his own anguish and ours by those cruel remembrances, he took another direction. During eight days he sought every spot where he had once wandered with the companion of his childhood. He traced the path by which she had gone to intercede for the slave of the Black River. He gazed again upon the banks of the Three Peaks, where she had reposed herself when unable to walk further, and upon that part of the wood where they lost their way. All those haunts, which recalled the inquietudes, the sports, the repasts, the benevolence of her he loved, the river of the Sloping Mountain, my house, the neighboring cascade, the papaw tree she had planted, the mossy downs where she loved to run, the openings of the forest where she used to sing, called forth successively the tears of hopeless passion; and those very echoes which had so often resounded their mutual shouts of joy, now only repeated those accents of despair, 'Virginia! Oh, my dear Virginia!'

"While he led this savage and wandering life, his eyes became sunk and hollow, his skin assumed a yellow tint, and his health rapidly decayed. Convinced that present sufferings are rendered more acute by the bitter recollection of past pleasures, and that the passions gather strength in solitude, I resolved to tear my unfortunate friend from those scenes which recalled the remembrance of his loss, and to lead him to a more busy part of the island. With this view, I conducted him to the inhabited heights of Williams, which he had never visited, and where agriculture and commerce

ever occasioned much bustle and variety. A crowd of
carpenters were employed in hewing down the trees,
while others were sawing planks. Carriages were passing and repassing on the roads. Numerous herds of
oxen and troops of horses were feeding on those ample
meadows, over which a number of habitations were
scattered. On many spots the elevation of the soil was
favorable to the culture of European trees: ripe corn
waved its yellow sheaves upon the plains: strawberry
plants flourished in the openings of the woods, and
hedges of rose bushes along the roads. The freshness
of the air, by giving a tension to the nerves, was
favorable to the Europeans. From those heights, situated near the middle of the island, and surrounded by
extensive forests, you could neither discern Port Louis,
the church of the Shaddock Grove, nor any other
object which could recall to Paul the remembrance of
Virginia. Even the mountains, which appear of various
shapes on the side of Port Louis, present nothing to
the eye from those plains but a long promontory,
stretching itself in a straight and perpendicular line,
from whence arise lofty pyramids of rocks, on the
summits of which the clouds repose.

"To those scenes I conducted Paul, and kept him
continually in action, walking with him in rain and
sunshine, night and day, and contriving that he should
lose himself in the depths of forests, leading him over
untilled grounds, and endeavoring, by violent fatigue,
to divert his mind from its gloomy meditations, and
change the course of his reflections, by his ignorance
of the paths where we wandered. But the soul of a lover
finds everywhere the traces of the object beloved. The
night and the day, the calm of solitude, and the tumult
of crowds, time itself, while it casts the shade of obliv-
ion over so many other remembrances, in vain would
tear that tender and sacred recollection from the heart,

which, like the needle, when touched by the loadstone, however it may have been forced into agitation, it is no sooner left to repose, than it turns to the pole by which it is attracted. When I inquired of Paul, while we wandered amidst the plains of Williams, 'Where are we now going?' he pointed to the north and said, 'Yonder are our mountains; let us return.'

"Upon the whole, I found that every means I took to divert his melancholy was fruitless, and that no resource was left but an attempt to combat his passion by the arguments which reason suggested. I answered him, 'Yes, there are the mountains where once dwelt your beloved Virginia; and this is the picture you gave her, and which she held, when dying, to her heart; that heart, which even in her last moments only beat for you.' I then gave Paul the little picture which he had given Virginia at the borders of the cocoa tree fountain. At this sight a gloomy joy overspread his looks. He eagerly seized the picture with his feeble hands, and held it to his lips. His oppressed bosom seemed ready to burst with emotion, and his eyes were filled with tears which had no power to flow.

"'My son,' said I, 'listen to him who is your friend, who was the friend of Virginia, and who, in the bloom of your hopes, endeavored to fortify your mind against the unforeseen accidents of life. What do you deplore with so much bitterness? Your own misfortunes, or those of Virginia? Your own misfortunes are indeed severe. You have lost the most amiable of women: she who sacrificed her own interests to yours, who preferred you to all that fortune could bestow, and considered you as the only recompense worthy of her virtues. But might not this very object, from whom you expected the purest happiness, have proved to you a source of the most cruel distress? She had returned poor, disinherited; and all you could henceforth have

partaken with her was your labors: while rendered more
delicate by her education, and more courageous by her
misfortunes, you would have beheld her every day
sinking beneath her efforts to share and soften your
fatigues. Had she brought you children, this would
only have served to increase her inquietudes and your
own, from the difficulty of sustaining your aged parents and your infant family. You will tell me, there
would have been reserved to you a happiness independent of fortune, that of protecting a beloved object,
which attaches itself to us in proportion to its helpless-
ness; that your pains and sufferings would have served
to endear you to each other, and that your passion
would have gathered strength from your mutual misfortunes. Undoubtedly virtuous love can shed a charm
over pleasures which are thus mingled with bitterness.
But Virginia is no more; yet those persons still live,
whom, next to yourself, she held most dear; her
mother, and your own, whom your inconsolable affliction is bending with sorrow to the grave. Place your
happiness, as she did hers, in affording them succor.
And why deplore the fate of Virginia? Virginia still
exists. There is he assured, a region in which virtue
receives its reward. Virginia now is happy. Ah! if, from
the abode of angels, she could tell you, as she did when
she bid you farewell. 'O, Paul! life is but a trial. I was
faithful to the laws of nature, love, and virtue. Heaven
found I had fulfilled my duties, and has snatched me
forever from all the miseries I might have endured
myself, and all I might have felt for the miseries of
others. I am placed above the reach of all human evils,
and you pity me! I am become pure and unchangeable
as a particle of light, and you would recall me to the
darkness of human life! O, Paul! O, my beloved friend!
recollect those days of happiness, when in the morning
we felt the delightful sensations excited by the unfold-

ing beauties of nature; when we gazed upon the sun, gilding the peaks of those rocks, and then spreading his rays over the bosom of the forests.

"'How exquisite were our emotions while we enjoyed the glowing colors of the opening day, the odors of our shrubs, the concerts of our birds! Now, at the source of beauty, from which flows all that is delightful upon earth, my soul intuitively sees, tastes, hears, touches, what before she could only be made sensible of through the medium of our weak organs. Ah! what language can describe those shores of eternal bliss which I inhabit forever? All that infinite power and celestial bounty can confer, that harmony which results from friendship with numberless beings, exulting in the same felicity, we enjoy in unmixed perfection. Support, then the trial which is allotted you, that you may heighten the happiness of your Virginia by love which will know no termination, by hymeneals which will be immortal. There I will calm your regrets, I will wipe away your tears. Oh, my beloved friend! my husband! raise your thoughts towards infinite duration, and bear the evils of a moment.'

"My own emotion choked my utterance. Paul, looking's at me steadfastly, cried, 'She is no more! She is no more!' and a long fainting fit succeeded that melancholy exclamation. When restored to himself, he said, 'Since death is a good, and since Virginia is happy, I would die too, and be united to Virginia.' Thus the motives of consolation I had offered, only served to nourish his despair. I was like a man who attempts to save a friend sinking in the midst of a flood, and refusing to swim. Sorrow had overwhelmed his soul. Alas! the misfortunes of early years prepare man for the struggles of life: but Paul had never known adversity.

"I led him back to his own dwelling, where I found

his mother and Madame de la Tour in a state of increased languor, but Margaret drooped most. Those lively characters upon which light afflictions make a small impression, are least capable of resisting great calamities.

"'O, my good friend,' said Margaret, 'me-thought, last night, I saw Virginia dressed in white, amidst delicious bowers and gardens. She said to me, 'I enjoy the most perfect happiness;' and then approaching Paul, with a smiling air, she bore him away. While I struggled to retain my son, I felt that I myself was quitting the earth, and that I followed him with inexpressible delight. I then wished to bid my friend farewell, when I saw she was hastening after me with Mary and Domingo. But what seems most strange is, that Madame de la Tour has this very night had a dream attended with the same circumstances.'

"'My dear friend,' I replied, 'nothing, I believe, happens in this world without the permission of God. Dreams sometimes foretell the truth.'

"Madame de la Tour related to me her dream, which was exactly similar; and, as I had never observed in either of those persons any propensity to superstition, I was struck with the singular coincidence of their dreams, which, I had little doubt, would soon be realized.

"What I expected took place. Paul died two months after the death of Virginia, whose name dwelt upon his lips even in his expiring moments. Eight days after the death of her son, Margaret saw her last hour approach with that serenity which virtue only can feel. She bade Madame de la Tour the most tender farewell, 'in the hope,' she said, 'of a sweet and eternal reunion. Death is the most precious good,' added she, 'and we ought to desire it. If life be a punishment we should wish for its termination; if it be a trial, we should be thankful that it is short.'

"The governor took care of Domingo and Mary, who were no longer able to labor, and who survived their mistresses but a short time. As for poor Fidele, he pined to death, at the period he lost his master.

"I conducted Madame de la Tour to my dwelling, and she bore her calamities with elevated fortitude. She had endeavored to comfort Paul and Margaret till their last moments, as if she herself had no agonies to bear. When they were no more, she used to talk of them as of beloved friends, from whom she was not distant. She survived them but one month. Far from reproaching her aunt for those afflictions she had caused, her benign spirit prayed to God to pardon her, and to appease that remorse which the consequences of her cruelty would probably awaken in her breast.

"I heard, by successive vessels which arrived from Europe, that this unnatural relation, haunted by a troubled conscience, accused herself continually of the untimely fate of her lovely niece, and the death of her mother, and became at intervals bereft of her reason. Her relations, whom she hated, took the direction of her fortune, after shutting her up as a lunatic, though she possessed sufficient use of her reason to feel all the pangs of her dreadful situation, and died at length in agonies of despair.

"The body of Paul was placed by the side of his Virginia, at the foot of the same shrubs; and on that hallowed spot the remains of their tender mothers, and their faithful servants, are laid. No marble covers the turf, no inscription records their virtues; but their memory is engraven upon our hearts, in characters, which are indelible; and surely, if those pure spirits still take an interest in what passes upon earth, they love to wander beneath the roofs of these dwellings, which are inhabited by industrious virtue, to console the poor who complain of their destiny, to cherish in the hearts of lovers the sacred flame of fidelity, to inspire a taste for the blessing of nature, the love of labor, and the dread of riches.

"The voice of the people, which is often silent with regard to those monuments raised to flatter the pride of kings, has given to some parts of this island names which will immortalize the loss of Virginia. Near the Isle of Amber, in the midst of sandbanks, is a spot called the Pass of Saint Geran, from the name of the vessel which there perished. The extremity of that point of land, which is three leagues distant, and half covered by the waves, and which the Saint Geran could not double on the night preceding the hurricane, is called the Cape of Misfortune; and before us, at the end of the valley, is the Bay of the Tomb, where Virginia was found buried in the sand; as if the waves had sought to restore her corpse to her family, that they might render it the last sad duties on those shores of which her innocence had been the ornament.

"Ye faithful lovers, who were so tenderly united! unfortunate mothers! beloved family! those woods which sheltered you with their foliage, those fountains which flowed for you, those hillocks upon which you reposed, still deplore your loss! No one has since presumed to cultivate that desolated ground, or repair those fallen huts. Your goats are become wild, your orchards are destroyed, your birds are fled, and nothing is heard but the cry of the sparrow hawk, who skims around the valley of rocks. As for myself, since I behold you no more, I am like a father bereft of his children, like a traveler who wanders over the earth, desolate and alone."

In saying these words, the good old man retired, shedding tears, and mine had often flowed, during this melancholy narration.

Printed in the United States
63846LVS00005B/127